FATALITIES AND FOLIOS

POE BAXTER BOOKS
BOOK 1

ACF BOOKENS

1

I looked at myself in the full-length mirror and lifted one corner of my mouth. The look was perfect, if a bit performative. A long velvet coat that cinched at my waist, black leggings meeting maroon boots that were not quite a match to the coat, and a top hat bedecked with a dark red ribbon. I looked just enough steampunk and just enough Victorian to take joy in my own attire. "Looking good, Poe Baxter," I said, reminding myself who I was.

This outfit was so different from my usual linen dresses or jeans with floral blouses. Today I was stepping into the bookish part of my persona, which felt ideal. This was, after all, the first day of my new career.

Just six weeks ago I had been an English professor, one whose teaching my students enjoyed (if their reviews were to be believed). I cared a great deal about my students – perhaps too much – but I had grown weary of committee meetings and esoteric discussions about literary theory. Even more, I had gotten tired of grading papers. Oh, so very tired.

So a year ago, I told my department chairs I was resigning. I didn't want to leave them with courses to cover and no new faculty member to teach them. Now, after a year that seemed it might never end, I was starting up my new business as a book finder. It was a job I'd never done before, but my Uncle Fitz assured me I'd be great at it given my literary knowledge and acumen for acquiring and retaining information. He would know. Uncle Fitz owned the most amazing rare book shop in Charlottesville, and as such he had been collecting books from all over the world for most of his seventy-five years.

"Girl, you are made for this work. It's in your DNA. I'm certain," he told me when he found out I was leaving teaching and looking for a new career. "I'm long past my traveling days, but with my experience and your knowledge of books, I think we can do quite nicely."

I had stared at him a little dumbfounded when he told me the salary he'd pay, a salary that outpaced my teaching one by a third, and when he added that he'd give me a commission for my finds as well, I almost refused, saying it was too generous. But then I took a deep breath, sat back into my worth like my therapist always said I should, and agreed.

"Now, we just need to pick your specialty. Let's see, I have buyers in contemporary fiction and the classics, and your friend Beattie has been indispensable in the eighteenth and nineteenth century European texts." He pushed a hand through his bushy gray hair. "How would you feel about finding folklore and fairy tale texts?"

How would I feel about it? I'd be overjoyed. I had studied those subjects in my PhD program, as Uncle Fitz well knew, and while I hadn't ever been hired to teach in those areas, they were still my passion. I just loved reading the stories that helped people from earlier times understand their lived experiences. Those tales helped me understand my experiences, too, even if I had yet to meet a dragon or a selkie.

I had looked at my uncle and rolled my eyes. "I guess I could handle that, Uncle Fitz." Then, I'd reached out and startled him with a huge hug. We weren't really the most physically demonstrative of families, but sometimes, the gifts in life required bone-crushing hugs. This was one of those times.

"Excellent, dear. Now, Beattie is already scheduled to go to Edinburgh for a bit of scouting about Stevenson first editions. Perhaps you'd like to join her?" He pulled a folder out of a tipping stack at the edge of his desk. "I got word of a rare collection of Scottish sea monster tales and thought that might be a good place to start." He handed me a photograph of a beautiful, leather-bound volume that featured a snake-like creature pressed into the front cover.

I stared at the blue leather and the fine work that had embossed it, and I nodded, unable to speak with my excitement. "When do we leave?"

My uncle grinned. "Friday. Beattie has all the information. She'll be your guide for our processes. I suppose you won't mind that." He winked at me.

Beattie Andrews was my best friend. Had been my best friend since second grade when she had walked up to me and said, "You look weird. I'm weird, too. Want to play dress-up?"

It was meeting of kindred souls from that day on. Even when Beattie had come out and begun her transition from male to female, we had stayed close even as a lot of our friends fell away because they just didn't know what to say or do . . . or because they were simply hateful. Through all the challenges she faced, Beattie was always there for me, through break-ups and two divorces, and now I was going to get to work with her. I was excited about the book collecting piece, but more, I was just excited to spend more time with Beattie.

And our first stop was Edinburgh, my favorite city (so far) in the world. I'd visited twice, once in college when the boy I loved and I sat on Arthur's Seat and surveyed the city below, and once after my mom died and a friend invited me over to enjoy the country with her and her family. On both trips, I'd

tried to take in as much of the Old City as I could, but I knew
I'd missed so much. And now, I could see all of it with Beattie.
Suddenly, forty-eight hours had seemed like a long time to
wait.

The days had flown by with packing and prepping our
contacts, a process Beattie had shepherded me through with
humor and style, and here I was donning my new but vintage
outfit for a plane ride. I knew Beattie would get a kick out of my
stylings, especially since she always looked effortlessly stylish
in her standard black leggings and tunics that highlighted her
willowy shape and long silver hair. She was not one to put on
airs, but today felt like an air-worthy day to me, and I was going
with it.

When I stepped out of my apartment building, Beattie was
at the curb in her white Subaru wagon. "Look at you," she said.
Without hesitation, she removed the hat from my head and
tossed it into the hatch of the car before moving out of the way
so I could put my small suitcase inside. She smiled at me
broadly. "You know you're just going to lose that before we get
on the plane."

I sighed. "Too much, huh?" I ran my fingers through my
thick curly hair. "It's probably for the best. This mess is going
up into a bun as soon as we're seated." I loved wearing my hair
down since I'd finally grown to love its massive volume, but it
was hot and hard to see through, so it was usually up on top of
my head as soon as it dried. Sometimes before.

"Not too much for our work, no. But yes, too much for the
plane. And you can't pack that thing." She climbed into the
driver's seat. "Love the jacket though."

I let a small smile pass my lips as I sat down beside her and
put on my seatbelt. "Me, too." I looked over at her, and as usual
she looked amazing, even in today's slight wardrobe deviation
of yoga pants and a t-shirt knotted at her waist. Her makeup
was flawless, and somehow her silver hair never had that

yellow tinge that seemed to affect other women's gray. "You wearing new blush?"

Her pale skin flushed as she pulled out onto Preston Avenue and started heading north of town toward the airport. "Do you like it?"

I nodded. "It gives you good color."

"I like it, too, and since it's that cream stuff, it feels moisturizing, too." She patted her cheeks. "Never enough moisturizer for my skin, you know?"

I did know. In this way we were about as different as could be. My skin went toward oily, and while I needed to moisturize as much as the next woman, I needed to keep things light to avoid breakouts. Beattie, however, seemed like she could lather on motor oil and never get a single pimple.

As we drove across town, I quizzed Beattie on what we were going to do (besides work) in Edinburgh. She had insisted on planning our itinerary, both bookish and tourist-ish, and she wanted it to be a surprise. I loved surprises, but I was also a person who liked to look up every detail of a new place before I visited. Beattie's closed lips meant I had had to wing it in my online reading. I knew a lot about Greyfriar's Bobby since I'd watched the movie and read the true story of the little loyal dog. I was sure Beattie would take us there since she knew I was a sucker for a good story, but beyond that, I was a loss.

My friend, however, was not spilling even a tidbit of our plans. She just kept saying, "I'll see."

"You hear her, Butterball," I said to the plump hamster tucked into his bespoke travel bag that Uncle Fitz had insisted on buying me as a "first adventure" gift. He knew I wouldn't be leaving my fuzzy pet at home, even if I found the best pet sitter in the world, especially since airlines didn't mind pets traveling as long as they had their paperwork.

BB was fully up to speed on his shots, had a microchip unless he wandered off, and was cleared for EU travel with a small passport-like document that I'd been able to procure online. BB had come to me sort of my happenstance when my neighbor's young daughter, Tilly, had decided the little guy would be happier outside in the wild. Fortunately, I'd been there to watch his first venture into the grass behind our building, and I'd kept a close eye on him until she went inside. Then, I'd scooped him up and taken him in with me, where I'd quickly spoiled him with all the best in hamster accommodations, including a rhinestone-encrusted running wheel that he refused to touch out of what, I am certain, was a desire to keep his round form in its most languid shape.

He did get regular exercise though because about once a week, I let him run around on Tilly's back porch while I kept an eye out for cats and hawks so that she could see he was happy and thriving in his new "wild" home."

Last night, when BB had made his trek to her deck, I'd let Tilly know that he had told me he was taking a vacation. She had clapped her hands and decided he must be going to a beach somewhere because, of course, that was her favorite vacation spot, a fact I simply didn't understand since I loathed the beach, especially in summer. Still, Tilly seemed satisfied with our tale of travel for the little rodent, and now, he was snoozing, belly up in his bag on my lap, clearly determined to ignore my attempt at conversation with him.

After I had tried to coax a peeved reaction from my pet and had been given only tiny snores, Beattie finally relented and said, "Okay, I'll tell you one thing. We are having afternoon tea at Edinburgh Castle tomorrow afternoon."

I squealed in delight, startling BB to an upright position, from which he stared at me with the kind of scorn only a hamster can muster. I didn't care. Afternoon tea in a castle. I couldn't wait.

· · ·

THE FLIGHT WAS PRETTY mundane except for the excellent coffee and the three small children who, despite BB's best imitation of a corpse, somehow figured out he was on the plane and made visits every half-hour or so to say hello. For his part, my pet acted the put-out divo quite well, but I could tell, as only I could, that he was secretly pleased with his new fan club. His tiny tail was puffed up quite a bit by the time we landed.

The children had been a delight, but as we got our bags and found a taxi to take us to the B&B Beattie had raved about on the flight, I felt myself growing fatigued. I hadn't ever really been one for all-nighters, and now, at 47, my body was definitely in opposition to them. And I knew that adjusting to the time difference after our overnight flight would be best achieved by staying awake all day.

Still, we had tea at the castle to look forward to, and if I knew Beattie, and I definitely knew Beattie, we'd be starting work right away. Fortunately, my best friend also had a hearty appetite, so she had pre-arranged a full English breakfast – I made a mental note to ask if there was such thing as a Scottish equivalent – upon our arrival at the B&B. Never had been I been so glad to see a sausage – a banger, I was corrected by my companion – as I was at that moment. The coffee on the plane had been wonderful. The rest of the food was sadly typical for air travel.

Breakfast in our tummies, our bags in our rooms, and our hostess cooing over Butter Ball in the front parlor, we set off to our first meeting of the day. As we walked toward the center of town and the National Library of Scotland, Beattie finally deemed me ready to hear our work itinerary. Apparently, our vacation one was still top-secret, to my continued annoyance.

"*The* foremost expert in Scottish folklore is meeting us today at 1:30. He has some insights about the book we're looking to procure from our meeting on Monday." She looked at me out of the corner of her eye. "Plus, he is single, as best I can tell, and quite your type." I tried to not look a little pleased, but given that my best friend knew just how abominable my dating experience had been in the past three years, I knew she wouldn't buy it if I tried to play it totally cool about a bookish, attractive man."

"Oh yeah?" I said with a strained attempt at casualness. "He's not your type?"

"Nope, not a beard or tattoo in sight." She grimaced. "Too uptight and brainy for me. So that means just perfect for you."

I could have argued, but she wasn't wrong. "So he knows about the Sea Dragon Chronicles, then." I had spent a fair bit of my time in the past two days looking up the various sea monster tales of Scotland and had been delighted to learn that they were thought to be a kind of dragon by some. Even old Nessie had some stories that linked her to fire breath. The laws of nature caused me to struggle with the idea of under-water animals breathing fire, but then again, I didn't under-stand how fish glowed in the dark, either, so I couldn't question much.

Beattie nodded. "He's done a fair amount of study about the lore, and while he has moved far past the point of believing in such animals, he does know a great deal about the people who created the legends. He told Fitz that this was the most exten-sive collection of medieval tales he'd ever come across and even hinted that he hoped the National Library might buy it."

I winced. "Oh no." I was suddenly even more nervous. "I don't want to be poaching national treasures from anyone, least of all a hot librarian."

Beattie shook her head. "Fitz made it clear that we were procuring the book for a Scottish patron who wanted to donate the book to the Library in honor of his father, a well-regarded Scottish paleontologist."

I sighed. "So the Library will get the book, but not have to buy it."

"Exactly," Beattie said with a grin. "Your uncle is famous in this industry for a reason."

She wasn't wrong. Uncle Fitz got commissions to find books all over the world, most for wealthy book collectors who wanted to add to their private libraries. But he was very discriminating in his choice of clients, so I should have known he would never be involved in anything that would be regarded as foul play by anyone in the business.

Uncle Fitz had two rules:

1. Books belong, when possible, available to the public in some form.
2. Books should stay at home as much as possible.

I knew he occasionally broke these rules when necessary, say when a book was in danger of being destroyed or lost and the only safe home he could find for it was in a country not of its origin. But by and large, he was devoutly faithful to his policies. It was one reason I was eager to work with him.

As we approached the library, I squashed the little bit of disappointment I felt at seeing the building. I'd been hoping for Scottish architecture with spires and arches, but instead, the building looked remarkably like the classic Greek architecture on which buildings in our own nation's capital had been fashioned. All clean lines and bare sandstone.

When we went inside, however, all my disappointment faded away as I looked at the illuminated manuscripts displayed in glass cases in the lobby. Each swirl and icon on the pages was hand-drawn, and I could have stayed to try and decipher the text all day.

But fortunately, or unfortunately as the case may be, my fascination with the manuscripts before me was interrupted when a very handsome, delightfully nerdy man in tweed and horn-rim glasses asked if I was Poe Baxter.

I stammered for a minute as I looked at him, and Beattie had to answer for me. "Yes, this Poe. I'm Beattie. Thank you for seeing us, Mr. Anderson."

"Adaire, please. Nice to meet you both," Adaire said in an accent that was definitely Scottish but also not quite the brogue I expected from my extensive experience with Scottish dialect derived exclusively from watching *Outlander*.

I finally put out my hand to shake his and pulled my face into a smile that I hoped seemed friendly and not like a creepy American stalker person. "Yes, thank you for seeing us."

"Are you a scholar of illuminated manuscript as well as folklore, Ms. Baxter?" he asked as he pointed at the glass case I had been staring at.

I blushed. He had called me a scholar, a title I was never afforded as a community college professor without a completed PhD. I was flattered but shook my head. "Far from it. I find the art to be fascinating, though, and the little I know about the practice of creating the illuminations is intriguing, too. Although I'll admit I learned most of that from Umberto Eco."

"Ah, *The Name of the Rose*," he said with a smile. "An excellent mystery." He blushed as little when he met my gaze. "Would you like more time here?" He glanced from me to Beattie.

I shook my head as I looked at my best friend, who had a knowing grin on her face that made me kind of want to punch her in the arm. "We can always come back. We want to respect your time." I smiled at him. "Plus, I'm so eager to see what you have to share."

He nodded, and Beattie and I trailed behind him as he took us to the back of the lobby and led us through an arched, wooden door. I was a sucker for a secret passageway, and this entrance very much felt like it could be one.

Unfortunately, that illusion dissolved a bit when the doorway opened onto a very typical corridor with doors on each side. What wasn't typical, however, was that the walls were covered in famous paintings, including a study for Da Vinci's "Virgin of the Rocks," one of my favorite paintings of all time. Without thinking, I stopped cold and stared at the woman's face and felt tears prick the back of my eyes.

Beattie stepped beside me and smiled. "She looks so wise, and a bit tired."

I sighed. "Yes, it's why I love the final painting. Da Vinci seemed to understand the weariness that comes from motherhood, even for the Virgin Mary."

Adaire turned back to us. "We hang some of the pieces that the National Gallery can't display." He gestured around the walls. "Everything is climate controlled here, so it's a good place for them. Plus, at least some people get to enjoy them instead of them living in storage for years at a time."

"It is a sort of aesthetic tragedy that so much great art sits in back rooms," Beattie said as we began to walk again. "Maybe we could take over a few superstores and turn them into museums."

That was a good idea, in my opinion, but I didn't have much time to think about it because Adaire led us through another door on the right side of the hall. The allure of magic around us again as we stepped into the wood-wall office. The walls were lined with bookshelves full of titles, and the large wooden desk was clear and polished, with just a laptop on it. The space seemed the opposite of my uncle's store, but somehow it felt just as vibrant, just as full of stories and their people.

As he took a seat behind his desk, he pointed to two wing-backed chairs in front of him, and Beattie and I sat down. The chairs were immensely comfortable, and I felt even more at home in this space as I noticed a small toy rabbit on the corner of a shelf behind Adaire's head. A man who could display a stuffed animal amongst all this heady, bookish stuff was my kind of man. I blushed at my own thoughts.

"Well, let's begin here," Adaire said as he pulled a slim folder from the shelf behind him. "This is the provenance, as best we can tell, for the book you are hoping to acquire." He spun the folder in my direction and slid it across the desk to me.

I leaned forward, opened the file, and stared at the image of the book at the top of the page. Definitely the same book. As I began to read, I found my pulse quickening. Apparently, the book had been handmade in Inverness in 1340 by a man named Angus Duncan. Duncan operated a small book bindery that supplied tomes to the clan chiefs of Scotland. Each book was one of a kind, the paper in front of me said, and each was immensely valuable because of its age and craftsmanship.

"The book contains all the seanchas about water monsters known at the time," I read. "*Seanchas*?" I asked Adaire. "Related to séances."

"In a way maybe," he said with a smile. "It's the Gaelic word for *lore*. I've always wondered how the term relates to the word *science* myself."

Beattie cleared her throat next to me, her not-so-secret way of signaling to me that we were about to go far off track. She knew that I could deep dive into etymology quite quickly if allowed. I glanced over at her and nodded and then flipped the page.

There, I saw a long list of names, beginning with Angus Duncan and moving through a whole slew of men up until 2019. The name listed there was Seamus Stovall, the man who currently owned the book. My uncle had told me a bit about Stovall, and while he sounded intriguing, he also sounded like a lot of wealthy white guys – very convinced that he had earned everything he had and, thus, required to be paid top dollar for it.

Still, my uncle and I shared the same biases about the

world, so I thought it wise to get Adaire's perspective on the current owner. "Tell me what you know about Stovall?"

Adaire rolled his eyes. "The word *eccentric* was probably coined for him. He has one of those mustaches that he waxes into curls at the end and then plays with as if they're his embodied talisman of good fortune."

"Wow. That's a wonderful description," Beattie said. "So he has a, uh, a strong sense of his self-worth?"

"That is kindly put," Adaire said with a smile. "He is incredible wealthy, and while he is also very generous with the small village he lives in, he's a shrewd businessman. He knows the monetary worth of this book and he will expect to be paid what he sees as his due."

I squinted at Adaire. "Your choice of words seems very deliberate there. " What he sees as his due?'"

Adaire raised his eyebrows. "Caught that, did you? Well, as I see it, this book is a national treasure, one that no one person can really own. But Stovall and I disagree on this point." He sighed. "It's one reason I was not able to acquire the book directly for the Library."

I nodded. "Well, I assure you our patron believes much as you do, and I look forward to returning the book to the public when we come back from the Highlands." I tried to sound confident, but for my first buying experience, it was beginning to feel a bit beyond my depth. "Is there anything further you'd like to be sure we know about the book?"

Here, Adaire leaned forward and raised one eyebrow. "Now that you ask, there is a legend about the book itself."

If my attention hadn't already been captured for a number of reasons by this conversation, this sentence would have brought me in completely. As it was, I mirrored Adaire's body language and leaned toward the desk. "A legend, you say?"

"A curse, really." Adaire spoke more softly. "The stories have it that the person who has possession of the book begins to see monsters in every body of water."

"Oh," I said as I imagined how I would feel if I saw a sea monster in every lake. I decided I might be more fascinated than anything, so I wasn't sure this story could actually be characterized as a curse. "Well, that would be disconcerting," I said, trying to be tactful, "but seeing monsters is something some of us might enjoy."

A glint of something between mirth and fear flashed through Adaire's eyes. "Agreed, if we were talking about monsters in only the lochs and oceans, but rumor has it that every man who has owned this book sees monster in *every* body of water he encounters." He laid hard emphasis on the word *every*.

"Like in his bathtub?" Beattie said quietly.

"And watering trough and pitcher and sometimes every mirror as well." Adaire's voice had grown somber.

I let out a long breath. "That's intense then, and maybe maddening in the very literal sense of the world." Seeing Nessie in the Loch was one thing. A monster in every reflective surface was another. "How does Stovall feel about this legend?"

"Now, I'm not implying anything at all about how you should go about your negotiations, you hear." He looked at Beattie and me with a firm gaze. "I'm just sharing what I've heard as potential background information. I have no part in how you acquire this manuscript."

I looked at Beattie, and we both looked back at Adaire and nodded. *Message received*, I thought.

He continued. "From what I've heard, Stovall has required his staff to cover all mirrors, has forbidden all standing water on his property, and makes his assistant do all internet work for him so that he doesn't even inadvertently see images of water on the screen." Adaire sat back and studied the two of us across from him. "From what I can gather, the previous owner's family became so concerned with his talk of monsters that they had him committed to a hospital for mental health treatment."

I stared at this man who had seemed, until this moment, quite reasonable and studied. "I want to be sure I'm understanding. You're saying this," I looked back at the list of names in front of me, "Davis MacDonald was diagnosed with a major condition that was caused - directly - by this book."

Adaire shook his head and smiled. "Not exactly. I'm not saying that's why he was diagnosed, or even that he was diagnosed with anything. What I am saying is that he claimed to be seeing monsters everywhere and that led his daughters to send him for treatment."

I whistled. "Alrighty then."

"So," Beattie turned to me, "what I'm thinking is that we need to talk to MacDonald's daughters to figure out exactly what they think happened with their dad. And then we can use that as leverage to help with our conversations with Mr. Stovall."

I nodded. "I think that is an excellent idea, Beattie. I'm glad you came up with it." I looked over at Adaire and winked. Then, we both blushed.

After exchanging numbers and making plans to follow up with Adaire after our trip to the Highlands, Beattie and I headed up to the castle for High Tea. On the way there, I studied the beautiful, old storefronts and tall houses along the road.

One particularly gorgeous building that was stuccoed in a pink that would have been garish anywhere but in this stony, gray city caught my eye. As we strolled past, I studied the beautiful wooden door and then glanced up to the lintel. There, carved in stone, was a sea monster, looking directly at me.

2

High tea was amazing, and I decided that when I made my millions, I was going to give everyone I love a chance for high tea once a week, at my expense. I loved it so much I decided I would even pay for the hours of work my people might lose if they came. It was that good.

However, as good as the scones and clotted cream were, they didn't completely shake the shivery creepiness I'd felt when I saw that sea monster carving. I wasn't believing in the myth, per se, but the fact that someone had been hospitalized was, at least in their mind, linked to a book I was trying to acquire had me a bit nervous. Plus, that monster had been scary, like it was a 2D gargoyle and I was a demon it was meant to repel.

So between the creepy factor, the full belly, and the jet lag, I was more than ready to go to sleep at 6 p.m. when we made it back to our B&B. Unfortunately, Beattie swore that would mess up my system more and insisted we visit a local pub for a pint and some "crisps" before we went to bed. While I wasn't sure what crisps were exactly and was totally sure I would fall asleep if I had more than one drink, I knew Beattie knew best and trudged behind her to a little pub up the block called "The Jolly Codger."

As it turned out, crisps were potato chips, and I was surprised to find that the bacon-flavored ones were particularly good. So good, in fact, that I had a second pint of cider to go with a second bag. It wasn't just the good food and drinks that were great in the pub, though. I could not get enough of the dogs beneath all the tables. In particular, I was enamored with a Scottish Terrier (of course) named Archie who kept bumping his head against my knee so I'd drop him a chip, er, a crisp.

Even Butter Ball was welcome in what turned out to be the local taxi drivers' hangout. A man named Henry saw him in his carrier, introduced himself to my hamster, and then proceeded to carry him around the pub and introduce him to all the fellows. Someone – probably multiple someones – slipped the little fluffball a bunch of cheese, and by the time he made his way back to me, he was passed out with all his feet in the air, like he had died from dairy delight.

But with all of us full and completely knackered, as the young guy at the bar had described the look on my face, both Beattie and I were ready to turn in for the night when a man in the corner began to tell a story about a sea creature called the stoor worm. Instinctively, I began to eavesdrop, and soon I found myself inching closer to hear more easily. When she realized we weren't actually going to sleep yet, my best friend took my arm, pulled out a wooden chair from a nearby table, and set me right next to the storyteller before planting herself on a window ledge nearby.

The teller's voice had as thick a brogue as I'd heard yet on our trip, and I kept having to pause my following of the story to figure out a few words from context. But he was a powerful storyteller. The gist of his tale was that this stoor worm was destroying villages and entire islands with its voracious appetite, so a clan leader offered the hand of his oldest daughter in marriage to the man who could kill the monster.

"A lad from me home, Orkney, volunteered for the job," the storyteller said. "And don't you know, he struck that worm down with a hoe."

I quirked my eyebrow at Beattie, who mouthed "a hoe?" I was just tipsy and exhausted enough to be unable to hold back a small laugh.

The storyteller turned to me. "Aye, Lassie. You think that's funny?" He scowled and then said, "Why do you think no one can find Nessie? Someone took her out with a rake." He winked and then threw back his head in laughter.

I flushed what I knew what have been a deep red but then I smiled and eventually started laughing, too, as the entire group around us began to chuckle. These men had suckered the two American women into a great joke, and I loved them for it.

When we all finished laughing, I said to the storyteller, "So the stoor worm, that legend is something people have told for a long time, isn't it?" I'd come across the story in my research and knew the Icelandic version of the tale was included in the book I was trying to buy.

"Aye," he said. "Lots of folks tell the tale. Just changes who did the killing and with what." He winked at me again. "Most Orcadians tell the tale of the boy who carried a burning bit of peat into the beast's belly and burned it from the inside out."

"Sort of like Jonah and the whale, but with monster hunting," I said.

The man looked at me askance for a brief moment and then said, "Precisely, lass. Precisely."

For the next hour, the fatigue was swept from my limbs as I listened to the men around us tell tales of selkies and dragons, ghosts and kelpies from their parts of Scotland. Each of the tale-tellers was different in brogue and style, but every one of them had such a natural flair for the telling that I began to wonder which demographic trait gave them the ability – their nationality or their profession. I expected it was some of both.

By the time Beattie and I dragged ourselves out the door, I was full of culture and story, cider and crisps, and I was certain my first trip to Scotland was not to be my last.

THE BEDS AT THE B&B felt like clouds given my level of exhaustion, and I slept hard all night, waking only when Beattie nudged me to say that if I wanted breakfast, I had fifteen minutes. She, of course, was up and dressed, makeup done and hair styled, and already fed. I stumbled downstairs with my hair in the messiest of buns and a sweatshirt thrown over my t-shirt and pj pants.

Our host came to the table in a kilt, knee socks, and a loose white shirt, and images of Jamie Fraser at age 70 came into my head. "Mornin,' Lass," he said in a far stronger accent than he'd had when we met him the day before. "On your first morn here, we always serve our most traditional fare."

"In your most traditional wear," I said with a smile.

"Indeed, Lass." He set a plate with sausage, tomatoes, toast, baked beans, and two eggs on it, and said, "I suppose you will tell me you'd like coffee."

I shrugged. "I am American, so yes. Thank you."

He winked at me and turned back toward the kitchen with a flourish just as Beattie sat down opposite me. "Eat up," she said with a wink.

The food looked amazing, even if I wasn't quite used to having tomatoes or beans for breakfast. The crisps from the night before had worn off, however, and I was starving. So I ate every bite, and three cups of coffee with heavy cream and sugar.

When I was done, my belly was perfectly full, and my excitement was growing. We were going to the Highlands today.

Beattie had her UK driver's license, and she'd already been out to pick up our rental car, a little Fiat that made my heart skip with even more enthusiasm. It was going to be a great day.

Our host bade us farewell and told us he looked forward to our return in a few days. "Don't be expecting to see me kilt again, though," he said with a chuckle. "That's just to put you in a wee bit of the Scottish spirit. Nessie will do the rest."

I laughed as we waved goodbye and stepped into our car for the drive north.

Once I got over the fact the expectation that we were going to die every time we got to a roundabout and went to the left instead of to the right like we did in the States, I relaxed and let myself get lost in the gorgeous landscape. It was rugged and vast, but not like the plains of the US, not like anywhere in America that I'd seen anyway. In some ways, it felt like coming home, which was a feeling I couldn't quite place since I'd never been here before. I figured it must have been some kind of epigenetic memory. My ancestors speaking to me through my cells.

About two hours into our trip, I started seeing signs for Loch Ness, and I begged Beattie to detour west and let us see the water – and hopefully the monster – before we finished our drive. She reminded me, however, that we had an appointment at 2. "If you'd gotten out of bed earlier, we might have been able to stop there, but as it is, we'll have to build that in after our work is done."

I sighed. She was right, but it didn't make me any less grumpy. And when, just outside Inverness, I saw signs for the Culloden battlefield, my mood worsened. We weren't going to have to time visit that famous site either, not now at least, and I didn't even ask my driver. She had on her serious face, and I wasn't about to press my luck with her mood. I needed her upbeat attitude to help me through this first client meeting in my new profession as a book acquirer.

My mood began to lift as soon as we entered the older city center at Inverness. A river ran right through the center of town, and I couldn't stop looking at the bridges that crossed back and forth across its span. It felt magical in a way I couldn't quite name, but it felt ancient and old. In that place, I found myself quite ready to also believe in sea monsters.

After grabbing a quick sandwich at a takeaway deli – cheese and butter on some of the best bread I've ever had – Beattie and I headed to our appointment at a local solicitor's office. Beattie had reminded me that lawyers were called solicitors here. "Don't get to snickering because of your association with all the crime shows that arrest people for 'solicitation,'" she cautioned with a firm gaze.

I had watched enough British crime dramas to know this, of course, so Beattie's caution only served to make me unable to think about anything else as we walked into the small house that served as the solicitor's office. But then, when I saw the red-headed, huge man behind the desk, I lost all train of thought because he looked precisely how I imagined a High-lander would look, the old TV show with the guy and the sword notwithstanding.

When Seamus Stovall stood up, he towered over me by more than a foot. His shoulders were almost double the breadth of mine, and when he shook my hand, I felt like a child putting my fingers into my father's meaty palm. He was gentle though when he greeted me, and while I now could see why the caber toss was not an impossible feat for some men, I found myself immediately liking the colossal man.

"Thank you for seeing us, Mr. Stovall," I said, suddenly concerned that there was some form of proper address besides "mister" that I was fumbling.

"You're welcome, Ms. Baxter," he said. "Thank you for traveling all the way up here to meet with me about our beloved book."

I smiled. Any man who called a book beloved was a friend to me. "My absolute pleasure. It's my first time in Scotland, and I love it here. Feels like a homecoming."

"Aye," he said. "You have roots here, I expect." His smile reached all the way to the edges of his crinkling eyes, but for just a moment, I saw the shrewdness that Adaire had been talking about at the Library. This man was kind, but not gullible. That I could already tell.

"Maybe," I said. "I'm one of those American mutts that has ancestors everywhere, I think." I was at a bit of a loss for how to carry the conversation forward from here, so I did what I'd learned in the classroom – I waited. Silence usually did a lot of work if you let it linger.

Unlike my students, however, Mr. Stovall didn't fidget. He simply reached below the desk between us and brought out a collection of photographs of a blue book, the cover of which was by now quite familiar. As he lay the photos on the desk, I leaned forward, eager to see more of the beautiful volume.

I SET the photos down on the table and took a deep breath. "It's a beautiful book, Mr. Stovall. If all is in order, I see no reason why our client might not be inclined to procure it. Given that, we can come to terms on a price and that we are able to see the actual book, that is." The one bit of clear advice Uncle Fitz had given me was that I should let the seller know, immediately, if the book met our standards and confirm that our interest was sincere, but under no circumstances was I to talk money until I had clear provenance.

Mr. Stovall's mouth tipped up at one corner, and once again, I saw that I was clearly negotiating with a man who knew the rules on these sorts of transactions innately. I was going to have to be at the top of my game.

"I'm glad you find the book to be what you expected. I am

prepared to retrieve it from secure storage for you, but in the meantime, here is a copy of the terms of sale from when I came to acquire the book. I cannot, of course, vouch for anything before my purchase, but given how many people know the book, I think you should be able to find that information easily enough." He passed me a sheet of cream-colored paper.

I picked it up and read the legal jargon that proved he had, indeed, bought the book from Davis MacDonald. He'd paid 25,000 pounds just four years ago. I was authorized to pay up to 40,000, so I assumed that this would be an easy conversation.

I should have remembered the saying about what happens when someone assumes.

"This looks to be in order," I said, passing the paper to Beattie, who had reviewed far more provenance documents than I had. "I'm prepared to offer you 30,000 pounds for the book if it is in the same condition it appears to be from the photos."

Stovall's eyes grew very wide, and he sat back so far in his seat that I thought he might tip over backward. "Ms. Baxter, I am certain you feel this is a generous offer, but the book, of course, is worth far more than that."

I kept my gaze steady while my brain whirled around what my next steps might be. My intuition lit on a memory from last semester when a young man had tried to negotiate a D in my class even though he had not turned in a single paper and had slept through most of class. "Ms. B," he'd said, "I'm a good guy. I made some poor choices this semester, but you know I know this stuff. You know I don't need to take this class again."

The student wasn't wrong. He did know the stuff. All the writing he'd done in class had been solid, very good actually. But having the knowledge and demonstrating the knowledge were not the same thing. He had failed and then egged my office door as a response. I had been furious and a bit hurt, but I had also reported him, and when the security footage from the office hallway had been reviewed, the student had been expelled. Demonstrating poor restraint and bad judgment had even more consequences than laziness, this man had learned.

However, this student had taught me two things that I could use in this moment as Mr. Stovall pushed to get more than he had demonstrated his item was worth. First, I didn't have to do anything in this moment because I had done what I had done well and in good faith. Second, arguing this point was not going to result in a better outcome, even if I went up to my full authorized offer of 40,000 pounds. From his reaction to my initial offer, he clearly thought the book to be worth far more -- perhaps exponentially more -- than I could offer, and given the wealth I could see displayed prominently around me, he wasn't in a position to need to sell.

I took a deep breath and said, "I see. Well, if I may, I'd like to take a couple of days, gather more research, and discussion the situation with our client. If it suits, I will come back on Friday to see the book in person and to provide you with our best and highest offer."

Mr. Stovall smiled and leaned forward. His kind expression was still there, but now, I could see the steely glint of victory and satisfaction behind his eyes. "Very well. I will look forward to continuing this discussion at the end of the week." He reached across the table, and I shook his giant hand.

"Thank you," I said and felt quite content to let him believe he had just successfully lobbed the first volley. In reality, my researcher's resolve had firmed up immensely, and I knew Beattie and I were about to go deep to find out more about this book so that either we could indeed offer more money, but still guarantee our client a great return on her investment. Or we could find out about anything that might make the book worth less than what Mr. Stovall believed it was. Either way, five days was a lot of time to find a lot of information.

· · ·

As Beattie and I walked back out onto the High Street of Inverness, I was feeling a swirl of emotions beneath my tornado of plans. I was a bit disappointed that I hadn't been able to secure the book in this first meeting, but my intuition was telling me there was much more to be had in many ways if we took our time here.

I was just turning to propose a plan to Beattie when a woman's voice called my name from behind us. When I turned, I saw a slip of a girl in jeans and a thick wool sweater jogging toward us. Her red curls were bouncing as she came toward us, and as soon as she got closer, I could see that she was kin to Mr. Stovall. She had the same kind, square face and strength, but in a tiny frame. "I'm sorry to bother you. Elsie Stovall." She put her out her hand, and I shook it.

"Nice to meet you, Ms. Stovall," Beattie said. "Did we just meet your father?"

"Uncle, actually. I spend summers here when I'm off from school in Edinburgh." Her smile was wide, and her accent was softer, somehow, than her uncle's. "I wanted to ask if he sold you the book."

I glanced at Beattie and then back at Elsie. "Don't you think that's something you should ask your uncle directly?"

She sighed. "I understand. I don't want to put you in an awkward position. I'll see if he'll tell me."

I studied her face a minute and had a sense that her way of "seeing" was going to be a little snooping in his office. "He doesn't share his business with you?" She was young, but not a child, maybe sixteen. Old enough to understand business, I figured, but then again, I didn't care for any children, so what did I know.

Elsie's face brightened. "Actually, most of the time he does, but not about the book." She shook her head. "Too many curses."

Once again, I looked at Beattie, and the small wrinkle

between her eyebrows deepened. "You believe in the sea monster curse?" she asked.

"I don't," Elsie said with a violent shake of her head. "But Uncle Seamus does. Very much so."

I frowned. "But if he believes the book curses who owns it, why didn't he want to sell it as quickly as possible?" I realized as soon as I spoke that I'd told Elsie just wanted she wanted to know.

She smiled. "Well, that's a good question. See, Uncle Seamus doesn't technically own the book. I do." She winked at me. "But since I am not of age yet, I cannot make my own decision about selling, you see." Her face grew somber. "If I could, I wouldn't sell, not for any amount of money. I'd simply donate it to the National Library. Let it go back where it belongs."

"So Seamus Stovall is your guardian?" Beattie asked.

"He is. You can think of me like his ward, the Scottish Jane Eyre." She smiled again, a glint of mischief in her eyes.

I shook my head. "I do hope this doesn't mean you've fallen in love with your uncle."

When the young woman's face blanched, I laughed. "You might want to read the book before comparing yourself to its heroine." I patted her arm. "Although, this book does seem a bit like Bertha Mason."

Beattie laughed, and then said to Elsie. "Jane Eyre's guardian Rochester keeps his insane first wife locked up in the top floor of their house."

Elsie looked puzzled for just a moment and then cackled. "That's exactly right." Then she turned to me, "But please, I'm not falling in love with my uncle. Ew."

This time, I laughed. "That's good to know for a number of reasons, Elsie," I said. Then, I looked her right in the eye and said, "I don't want to put you in an awkward position, but if your uncle believes this book is cursed, doesn't it seem a bit cruel to leave you with the curse when he could get you out from under it?"

Elsie sighed. "He doesn't see it that way. I don't believe the curse, you see, and I definitely don't feel plagued by sea monsters. Uncle Seamus has decided it's because I'm not of age yet and, thus, am not affected."

Beattie rolled her eyes. "That's a lot of mental gymnastics to get himself more money." Then she winced. "Sorry. I didn't mean to speak ill of your uncle."

"No, that's what most people think about him. He does care about money, but only inasmuch as he can use it to help other people." She moved her gaze from Beattie to me as she said, "He's paying for my education as far as I'd like to take it, and he does the same for all the children of people on his staff. Plus, he gives a great deal to various charities. His goal is not to get rich, but instead to share his wealth."

I studied the girl's face for a moment, trying to decide whether she was well-informed or incredibly naive. I decided to go with informed only because it felt better to believe that both about her and her uncle. "All right, then, so we'll just have to see if we can get Uncle Seamus his due for this book," I said to Beattie.

She nodded, slowly. "Any tips on things we should look into?"

A slow smile spread across Elsie's face. "Well, if you want my opinion." She paused and looked from Beattie to me.

We both nodded, and she continued. "I'd start with Mr. MacDonald, the man who sold Uncle Seamus the book. He knew loads about it, and he believed in the curse. I mean, he really believed in it." Her eyes grew wide, and she sighed. "Sometimes he doesn't make much sense, but when he does, it's fascinating."

"You've talked to him?" I asked with surprise.

"Oh yes, many times. He lives just over the hill in Dalneigh.

Loves visitors, but don't call ahead. His nurse is a cretin and won't let you in." She dug into her pocket and pulled out a receipt wrapped around a lip gloss, unscrolled it, and scribbled out MacDonald's address on the back. "You'll let me know what you find?"

Beattie and I exchanged a look. "If your uncle says it's okay, absolutely," I said. "We'll be back on Friday at two. Maybe we'll see you?" This was the best I could do to give her information without betraying her uncle's trust.

"Oh, definitely. I'll plan on it," she said. Then she turned and walked back toward her uncle's house.

"Well, that was a good bit of information to gain on the sidewalk," I said.

"The pavement, Poe. They call it the pavement here," Beattie said as she slipped her arm through mine.

I rolled my eyes and let her lead me back to our car.

Despite my eagerness to meet with Mr. MacDonald right away, Beattie insisted we slow down, strategize our plan for the week, and have a pint. "Let's enjoy the town a bit and get our bearings."

I sighed. She was right, but I was never one to plan. I liked to charge ahead and live with the consequences, good or bad. That life philosophy had gotten me into trouble more than once, and more often than not that trouble had meant Beattie needed to rescue me. Her desire to slow down would save me some pain and her a whole heck of a lot of trouble.

We checked into our new B&B for the night, and once again, the bed began calling to me as soon as I saw it. The loss of an entire night's worth of sleep was weighing heavy, but when Beattie reapplied her lipstick, tossed me a sweater, and dragged me out the door for dinner, I didn't resist. She was a world traveler and the best foodie I knew. If dinner was in the plans, I wasn't going to miss out on what Beattie picked.

And I wasn't disappointed. She had located a quaint restaurant in a refurbished church. They had a great wine selection, and the food was delicious and all locally sourced. Our table was up on a wrought-iron balcony overlooking the River Ness, and by the time I had begun sipping my second glass of wine, I was absolutely enamored with this city.

While something in my gut was saying the meeting with Davis MacDonald wasn't going to be my favorite hour of the next day, I was glad the need to visit him had required another day in this town. The bridges across the river were lit with golden bulbs, and I could almost imagine the Loch Ness Monster, or her children, swimming upstream just to celebrate in town once in a while.

After finishing up the best Crème brûlée I'd ever had, Beattie and I decided to take a walk and enjoy the city. It was one of those places where it seemed like time overlaid itself. At moments, I felt like I was in a medieval town with the stone walls and cobbled walkways. The castle, of course, helped solidify that impression.

But sometimes, I also felt like I was in a modern city with the bright storefronts and crowded side--, I mean pavements. The night was chilly, and the more of the warm pub doors we passed, the more I was longing for a night like the previous one where we could enjoy some stories and maybe a cider or two.

When we circled back toward the center of town, I convinced Beattie to step into a place called MacCallum's, and we both immediately smiled when we stepped in. The place was filled with live music and laughing people, and when we got two pints and took a table in the corner, I felt myself relax even further. There was just something about a classic pub that we didn't have in the US, at least that's what my two nights' worth of experience was telling me. The coziness. The community. Even the best dive bars in the oldest neighborhoods in American cities just didn't compare.

The two of us sat for a while watching the band play. The music was good – sort of folksy with a drummer behind it – and if I hadn't been so tired, I might have wanted to stay longer. But again, the sleep was catching up with me, and when I looked to Beattie, she gave me the nod. It was time to go.

I stood, a little wobblier on my feet than I had expected, and almost fell over the chair behind me. When I righted myself on the shoulder of the man whose lap I'd almost landed in, I was surprised to see Adaire Anderson looking up at me.

"Oh, hi, Adaire," I said as I felt my face flush. He looked even more handsome than before in a dark green sweater and khakis.

Beattie stepped up behind me and subtly removed my hand from the man's shoulder. "How interesting to see you here, Mr. Anderson," she said as she shook his hand and then nodded to the other man at the table.

"I suppose it does seem odd," he said as he looked from her to me. "But I am from here in Inverness and come back as often as I can. This is my brother Arran. Arran, meet Poe and Beattie." He gestured to each of us in turn. "We met this weekend to discuss an acquisition for the Library."

I took Adaire's offhand way of describing our conversation as a signal to leave Arran out of the details. But my curiosity was piqued. It seemed far too coincidental that we'd run into Adaire -- not only in Inverness but in the very pub we had chosen for our evening's entertainment. And if he didn't want to talk about the book in front of his brother . . .

"Arran is a fisherman, lives out on Skye," Adaire said as if reading my mind and giving me an explanation in response to my skepticism. "My work bores him to tears, so we make it a point to not talk fish or old papers when we get together before he heads off for the main season."

"Please sit," Arran said in a deep, rich voice. "Let me get you another pint."

I looked over at Beattie to see what she was thinking about this invitation, but she was already taking the chair nearest Arran. And the flush in her own cheeks made me think she might have more than just a desire to be civil in mind as a reason to stay.

While Arran went to the bar, I turned to Adaire and said, "Did I forget you were from Inverness?" I knew right well I hadn't forgotten. I only knew about five places in Scotland, and if Adaire had told us he was from the next town we were visiting, I would have remembered.

"Oh, no, I don't think I said anything. Seemed a little selfish to push my love for my home on you when you were coming up for business." He slid his chair a bit closer in toward the table, and thus to me, "but I can't say as I'm sad to have run into you. Or for you to have run into me, rather."

I blushed and laughed. "It is a nice surprise. So you said you came up because your brother is leaving? Did I understand that right?"

"Aye," Adaire said just as Arran came back with the pints and set them on the table. "Aaran fishes crab, and the last month of the season is coming up."

Aaron nodded as he swallowed almost half his pint in one gulp. "But no one wants to hear about me and a boat, Ade," he said.

Beattie leaned way forward and tilted her body toward Arran. "I do," she said with a bit more breath in her voice than usual.

I looked over at Adaire, who winked conspiratorially at me. A flush of heat spread from my shoulders up to my scalp, and I winked back. Then, I turned to him and asked him to tell me what we should do with our final afternoon in Inverness.

Two hours later, I had a whole plan for museums and

galleries that would allow Beattie and me to enjoy what I now thought of as Adaire's city and region and let us meet up with the two men for dinner on our way back to Edinburgh. As the brothers walked us out, I tried hard to keep both my head and my body level. I was feeling swoony in a lot of ways, and I was determined not to embarrass myself.

3

———

Fortunately, when I woke up in the B&B the next morning, I could remember all of the night's events, and I didn't think I'd done anything embarrassing like declare my undying love for a librarian I'd only seen twice in my life.

Unfortunately, my crush did get the better of me at breakfast when I told my best friend I was excited about the double date we'd planned. She rolled her eyes and said, "You do remember we live in the States, and these two men are fully grounded here in Scotland, right?"

I did remember, but I had been trying to forget. "Of course," I said, "but stranger things have happened."

"In Hallmark movies, Poe. Hallmark movies. Unless you're planning on opening a Scottish-themed soap shop back in Virginia, I think it's best we consider tonight an evening with new friends." She sounded adamant, but I could see the shadow of disappointment on her face. "Right?"

"What if we thought about it as a date, but just a casual one?" I suggested. "Friends but with flirting."

This brought a smile to her face. "I like that plan. But now, we need to get serious. What are we trying to find out from Davis MacDonald?"

Now, it was my turn to get serious. "Well, it sounds like he may be contending with some mental struggles, so I'm trying to keep my expectations reasonable. But I'd like to confirm how much he sold the book to Stovall for, and I'd like to know what he paid for it, if he'll share. I'd also like to hear more about this curse, from his point of view, see if that might provide a bit of a tool we can use when we go back to the table with Stovall."

Beattie nodded. "Hopefully, he's forthcoming," she said with not a small amount of skepticism in her voice. "But just in case, let's fortify with a little tea and shortbread on the way."

I looked down at the plates we'd just cleaned of an entire English breakfast, rubbed my belly, and said, "Sounds good."

With directions to a local bakery from our host, we headed out into the busy streets of Inverness. I was always curious about the way cities held different energies. There was a similar frenetic undercurrent everywhere, but in New York, for example, the energy was pointed, focused, with everyone intent on where they were going. Our small city, Charlottesville, was airier and more open; forward-looking but with an undercurrent of arrogance bred by long history. Inverness, though, Inverness felt more staid in its history, confident about itself without having to prove anything. She reminded me of older women I knew who were kind but brokered no fools and who carried themselves with a quiet dignity that flowed through everything they did. A staid, strong, graceful lady. Maybe this is why I was falling in love with the city.

Well, that and the shortbread. Seriously, shortbread is a great gift to the world.

Our cups of tea and scone-size pieces of shortbread in hand, Beattie and I made the walk across town and up into Dalneigh and used our phones to locate MacDonald's street. It was beautiful in a sort of midcentury European way. Not to my taste as much as, say, the Cotswolds in southwestern England, but still charming and just different enough from the midcentury suburbs of America to feel new.

MacDonald's house was sort of moderate in size for the street, and when we opened the gate at the front garden, I grinned at the beautiful array of flowers and shrubs he had in place instead of a yard. The space was a perfect "cottage garden," and not for the first time, I found myself wondering if I could do that with my little apartment yard back in Charlottesville. Then, I wondered what my neighbors, staunch lawn mowers and herbicide sprayers, would think.

I didn't have much time to weigh my options there, though, because Beattie was striding toward the door with a grace I was never going to master in heels. She'd tried to teach me, but Danskos were always going to be my preference over anything that elevated the back of my foot far above my toes.

She stepped onto the small sandstone stoop and raised her hand to knock, but as she did, the door swung open of its own accord. I stepped up behind her and peered down the long hallway lined with dark wood paneling of a craftsman style. It was beautiful, and I was tempted to just walk in. But Beattie put her hand on my arm and held be back. "Poe," she whispered as she directed her gaze just to the right of the front door.

There, framed in an opening, was a pair of fine leather loafers with the toes pointed upward, which I could tell were the ends of a pair of legs in tweed. I sucked in my breath and said quietly, "We need to see if he's alive." I strode into the room, even as Beattie hissed at me to stop and pointed out that I might be disrupting a crime scene.

I realized that, but if this man was still alive, I wasn't going to just stand at the door and watch him – or at least his feet – die. I stepped beside him and saw an older man with silver hair and a very impressive mustache thick enough to make Wilford Brimley jealous. He wore round glasses, and I imagined that before the gray pallor of death had settled over him, he'd had rosy cheeks.

Now, though, he was quite gray. Before I even put my fingers to the part of his neck where I thought I might feel his pulse, I knew he was dead. The clammy skin beneath my pointer and middle fingers confirmed it. He was dead, very dead.

I quickly backtracked to the front door and said, "We need to call the police."

"No need," a deep voice said from behind us. "Would you like to tell me what you're doing here?"

Beattie's and my eyes met, and I could see panic that matched mine in her eyes. But we both turned and looked at the barrel-chested man dressed all in black and with close-cropped brown hair and deep brown skin behind us. "We were just coming to visit Mr. MacDonald," Beattie started. "But I'm afraid he's dead."

The police officer studied us a minute. "Did you open the door?" he said as he peered behind us.

"No, sir," I said in a far squeakier voice than I would have liked. "When we went to knock, the door swung open." I swallowed hard. "I did step inside to check on him. He's definitely dead." I braced myself for a scolding or, worse, handcuffs, but the officer gave one crisp nod.

"Please wait here," he said and strode past us to the front door, where he looked inside with a studied gaze and then walked slower to where the body lay.

As the officer knelt down, Beattie had the wherewithal to suggest we step back a bit, so we moved to a small bench just off the walkway. If I hadn't been so unnerved by the events of the last few moments, I might have enjoyed looking at MacDonald's fine garden. As it was, I could barely register that he seemed to have a penchant for lilies.

Beattie and I sat close together, completely quiet, even as neighbors began to gather on the street, apparently drawn over by the combination of the police car at the curb and the presence of two strange women in MacDonald's yard. No one spoke to us, though, which I appreciated and chalked up to another thing that the Scots had over the Americans. If we'd been at home, at least three people would have already asked us what was going on. I preferred the Scots' quiet nosiness to the more abrasive American version.

After a few minutes, another police car arrived, and two women went inside the house after giving their own brisk nods in our direction. Beattie looked at me and said, "Odd how trusting of us they are, isn't it?"

I nodded. "Maybe we just look trustworthy."

"I rather think it might just be that it's fairly easy to track down two Americans in Inverness," a woman from over the fence said with a gentle smile. "I heard you were in town yesterday."

I smiled at her and nodded, figuring she was right. "You may have a point there," I said, hearing the tiniest bit of brogue slip behind my Southern American accent. I knew I'd hear about my tendency to pick up accents from Beattie later. She always teased me about it, although I couldn't help it. I chalked it up to the theater classes I took in college and all the coaching the dialect expert had given me when everything I said had a slight Virginia drawl.

The first officer came back out and headed for us. "You were right, Miss, Davis is most definitely dead. Thank you for checking on him, though. Poor fellow didn't deserve to die that way."

Before I could think, I said, "What way is that, Officer, um--?" I found myself stumbling over both the man's rank and his name.

"Inspector Scott," the officer said, "and I'm afraid I will have to refrain from further comment on Davis's death, Miss?" He raised an eyebrow.

"Baxter," I said, "Poe Baxter, and this is Beattie Andrews." I started to tell him why we were there but thought better of it when I remembered Uncle Fitz's caution about revealing more than necessary.

"You're staying downtown, I understand," said Inspector Scott, and I caught the eye of the woman beyond the fence again as she gave me a small nod. "May I call on you there later if I have further questions?"

I hadn't had a lot of formal conversations with police officers in the US, but I could not imagine any of them asking permission to question us later. "Sure. Would you like our number?" I asked.

"No need. If it suits, I'll plan to meet you in the lobby of the hotel at four for a cuppa and a chat," the inspector said.

"Perfect, Inspector," Beattie said as she stood and stretched out her hand. "We'll see you then."

Following her lead, I stood and walked beside her to the sidewalk, where the neighbors stepped away to let us pass without a word.

AFTER WE HAD WALKED a couple of blocks, Beattie said, "We might need to get our story straight about what we're going to share and what we're not."

I stopped walked and turned toward her. "You're thinking of not telling him something about the book?"

"I'm not sure," she said. "He seems trustworthy enough, but we don't know why Davis MacDonald was killed. But given the curse—"

"Are you serious?" I said far too loudly. "You actually believe in that thing?"

Beattie tilted her head and looked at me like I'd just suggested she actually eat fast food. "No, Poe, I don't. But it isn't about what I believe. If that inspector believes in the curse, it will affect how he investigates, now won't it?" Her tone was just the teensiest bit patronizing, but I saw her point.

"Fair enough, so how do we play this?" I asked as we resumed our walk back downtown. "Do we act like we believe or act skeptical?"

A twinkle came into Beattie's eye, and she said, "How about both?"

I looked at her out of the corner of my eye. "Only if I get to be the true believer."

"I wouldn't have it any other way," she said.

A FEW HOURS LATER, after we'd both had lunch from a local takeaway place and had succumbed to a nap on the very soft beds in our room, Beattie and I made our way down to the hotel lobby and waited for Inspector Scott. As I watched the people come In and out of hotel, I thought of how "on the nose" the inspector's name was, a Scott from Scotland, but then I remembered that the renovation celebrities Drew and Jonathan were also named Scott and wondered if it was common, like the way Smith was a named derived from blacksmith.

My mind began wandering even further afield as I thought about whether the Scott brothers might ever come to Charlottesville for a job, then I supposed that if they did, that salvage expert from nearby Octonia, Paisley Sutton, might get to be involved, which would be awesome since I loved her newsletter and her stories about her young son.

Soon, my mind was constructing an elaborate story where Paisley became the newest member of the Scott family, perhaps by marrying Jonathan, and they moved to Charlottesville to begin renovating all the old buildings around town and making them affordable for low and middle-income people. I had gone into full-blown fantasy mode when Beattie elbowed me hard in the side and said, "Poe, stop daydreaming. He's here."

I followed her gaze to where the inspector was striding purposefully in our direction. He looked pleasant enough about the face, but something about the length of his stride made me think he was all business. "Ladies," he said as she sat down on the bench perpendicular to ours. "Thank you for meeting me. This shouldn't take long."

We had nowhere to be, but I hoped he was right. I didn't really love being questioned about a death on which we could give no insight.

"So let's begin with the obvious. Why were you at Davis MacDonald's house earlier?" he said casually as he drew a small notebook out of his pants pocket.

Beattie took that first question. "We were going to inquire with Mr. MacDonald about a book he had recently sold. We are book buyers, you see." Her tone matched the inspector's, and I hoped he didn't take the way she shifted in her seat as a sign of duplicity, especially since she was telling the full truth.

"And what book was that?" he asked.

"It's a collection of sea monster stories," I said. "Forgive my Gaelic, but it's something like Finseal Oilfist."

The inspector's face broke into a wide smile. "That was very good, lass. The Finscéal Ollphéist, a famous book indeed."

"You've heard of it?" Beattie asked with far more innocence than she actually possessed.

"Well, of course I have. It's cursed, you know." He winked at Beattie then.

She nodded with exaggeration and said, "Of course it is."

The game was afoot. "You don't believe in the curse," I said, trying to sound a little upset by the idea.

"I don't believe in anything I can't see with my own two eyes, be that sea monsters or curses," the police officer said. "But I take it you do."

I shrugged, trying to look like I was feigning disbelief. I found it a psychological challenge to pretend to be disinterested in something I was pretending to be interested in, but not really interested in. "Maybe?" I said.

"Why is that?" the inspector said in what seemed like an innocent and polite tone but that, I suspected, indicated a much deeper question than appeared on the surface.

"So many people who have owned the book have died, and now the curse has taken Mr. MacDonald, too," I lowered my voice to a half-whisper. "It would suit me just fine if we couldn't buy the book and just headed home without it."

"I see," he said and shot a wink to Beattie. "So you think the curse killed Davis?" He looked back at me.

"Well, I don't think the curse actually killed him, if that's what you mean. That kind of magic only happens with the darkest witches," I was leaning hard into my role now. "But someone under the curse's influence might have."

"So you think it was murder?" he said as he looked down at his notepad and then up at me from beneath his eyebrows, as if his question was not quite casual.

But as soon as I'd said it, I'd known I was right. I wasn't sure how, but I'd known since the moment I knelt over his body that Davis MacDonald had been murdered. "I do," I said, figuring at this point honesty was better than role-playing.

"Well, you'd be right," he said. "Any idea how he died?"

I studied the inspector's face, and he kept his eyes on mine. "He was hit in the head," I said, surprising myself. I hadn't realized I'd deduced that, but I knew it was soon as the words left my mouth. "I saw the blood and the damage to the side of his skull, I think."

"Good lass," he said. "If you hadn't mentioned that, I would have had reason to be suspicious." He smiled. "You had me a bit worried when you asked about the cause of death earlier."

This time, I was puzzled. "But you gave me the benefit of the doubt anyway?"

"Sometimes it takes a bit for these things to sink in past the shock. Seems that's the case here, too." He looked over to Beattie and then back at me. "Anything else you've remembered? Anything at all that seemed out of place?"

I looked at Beattie, and then we both shook our heads. "Not that comes to mind, Inspector," Beattie said. "But of course, we are not from here, so it would be hard for us to know what was out of the ordinary."

"Fair enough," he said. "Any how did you know to talk to Davis about this book of yours?"

I briefly explained about our conversation with Stovall and his desire to obtain far more for the book than we had been prepared to pay. "We had hoped to get some clarity on the book's value from Mr. MacDonald."

"Ah, very good." The inspector stood up. "I think I have all the information I need, but in case I come upon anything about the book that might be of interest to you, will you be here a while?"

"We're heading out into the Highlands and the Isle of Skye tomorrow, but you have our numbers, and we will be back in Inverness by the weekend," Beattie said before adding, "Anything in particular we should see out that way?"

"Well, given your project here, you'll definitely want to visit the Loch Ness Museum and see if you can spot the old girl herself, but personally, I'd recommend Eilean Donan castle. Bonny bit of landscape that one." He gave us a quick two-fingered salute. "Safe travels."

As we watched him walk out the door, I felt a growing affection for the inspector. "I like him," I said to Beattie.

"I do, too," she said. "He doesn't miss a thing, but he also doesn't assume a thing either. I like that in a person."

OUR BUSINESS CONCLUDED and we had a couple hours to kill before our dinner reservations at another quaint restaurant

Beattie had found, we headed back to our room to pick up our traveling companion and take him out for a bit.

Most people did not think of hamsters as good travelers, and I can't speak for others. But BB travels like a seasoned voyager. He's quite adaptable to any environment, and he loves sight-seeing, especially from the translucent plastic bag that Beattie had custom-made for him. It had a sheepskin floor, several ventilation holes for oxygen flow and temperature control and a small water bottle suspended in one corner. Every time I put BB in it, I thought of the Pope and his Popemobile. I knew it was sacrilegious, but I was seriously thinking of getting BB a white cassock and one of those pointed hats that the pope wears for formal occasions.

This afternoon, the sun had come out on what was apparently a rare event in Inverness if the comments and looks of awe and delight on the townspeople were to be believed. Several people were walking around with their hands out and their faces turned up to the sky as if they'd been living in an underground community for decades. It was pretty fun to see.

BB was similarly excited, but his joy took the form of sprinting back and forth across his bag so that he could see everything from every angle. As usual, he was also the source of much amusement, and Beattie and I spent the better part of our quite short walk answering questions about the hamster and pointing out that it would not be wise to take him out to hold him on the open street since he might fall.

What we did not say was that Butterball was quite likely to bolt for the closest scent of food that he could find. Every time we took him outside, I feared he'd be able to pull back the zipper, bust open the snap, and leap from his bag to go let himself into a restaurant kitchen, where the chef would find him making his own food a la Ratatouille.

Today, we made it about two steps at a time as people caught sight of our chubby brown critter and asked everything from his name to where they could acquire one. My knowledge of pet stores was fairly limited even in the US, so I had nowhere to direct them. One woman seemed particularly put out that I could not recommend a reputable shop in Inverness for her, and I made a mental note to ask our concierge about options before we took BB out in the Highlands. I didn't want to be the cause of such pet-related scorn again.

While I was flummoxed by the attention, Beattie became, as usual, more graceful and charming. With each stop and query, she seemed to become more and more like the 1920s Hollywood actress I secretly thought she must have been in another life. She'd slow down her speech and get more languid in her movements, even as her radiant beauty got more and more noticeable, as if the sun was turning just to get her into the perfect light. I'd told her about this phenomenon on several similar occasions, but she just laughed and suggested I be a little less dramatic. She was one to talk.

We were just about to head back to the hotel and return BB to his travel cage so that he could nap away the excitement when a tall, reedy woman with a thatch of dark hair and a sort of awkward gait approached. Given that we had just spent the last hour as the spokeswomen for our hamster, I figured this woman was going to want to see him up close, so as she approached, I lifted his bag higher so she could get a better look.

But instead of focusing her eyes and the requisite cutesy voice on our tiny companion, she met my gaze and thrust out a hand. "Ma- Andrea MacDonald," she said. "I wanted to thank you for finding my father and calling the authorities this morning."

I started to correct her and tell her we hadn't, indeed, called anyone, wouldn't have even known how to do so, when the weight of Beattie's hand on my arm made me hold my tongue.

"I'm so sorry for your loss, Ms. MacDonald," Beattie said before stepping forward to hug the surprised woman.

Ms. MacDonald extricated herself from the clearly unwanted display of sympathy and, straightening her denim vest, said, "Thank you. But we weren't close."

Now, I'd heard people say this on movies and TV shows before, and I'd always chalked it up to a bit of poor writing since it seemed like a sort of shorthand for letting the audience know that the two characters didn't have a good relationship. Now, though, I found the declaration remarkably disturbing because it was profoundly callous and completely unnecessary.

"I'm sorry to hear that," Beattie said. "But he was your father all the same." I could hear the slight reproof in Beattie's voice, but I wasn't sure it got through to Ms. MacDonald.

"He was, and well . . ." Ms. MacDonald's voice trailed off before she finished her sentence. I got the impression she'd thought better of finishing it. "Might I ask why you were visiting him today? He hasn't been well for quite some time, and I am under the impression that he didn't receive many guests."

I wanted to ask how she might have come to that impression if she wasn't speaking with her father much, but I decided to simply pin up that query for a later day. "We wanted to speak with him about a book he recently sold," I said instead.

Ms. MacDonald's entire posture stiffened, and it took her a minute to pull her poise together and ask, "Oh, he sold a book recently? I wasn't aware." She tossed the ends of her not-really-tossable hair and said, "Out of curiosity, which book?"

Beattie spoke over me as I started to tell her the name. "I'm afraid we're not at liberty to discuss that with anyone but our client and their approved list of parties," Beattie said. "You understand?"

Given the shade of pink that spread up Ms. MacDonald's face, I didn't think she understood at all, but she had the grace not to say so. "Very well, then. Again, I just wanted to thank you." She shook each of our hands briskly and then turned on her heel and headed back the way she came, her walk even more stiff than it had been when she arrived.

Beattie, BB, and I made our way back to the hotel as briskly as we could, with BB tucked under my arm to protect him from his adoring fans, and once we were back in our room, I said, "Okay, that whole Ms. MacDonald thing was weird, right?"

"So weird," Beattie said as she placed BB in his cage so he could collapse in the corner from exhaustion. "She was definitely fishing for information."

"Definitely, and did you see her reaction to the fact that we wanted to talk to her dad about a book?"

"If he was even her dad," Beattie said.

I gasped. "You think she was an impostor?" As if a murder and a cursed book weren't enough, now we had spies. "Do you think she was wearing a disguise? Like maybe that wasn't her real nose?"

Beattie, once again, rolled her eyes. "I *think* we should tell Inspector Scott about our encounter. Let him do his work and investigate."

I sighed. She was right, of course, but also, where was the fun in doing the right thing? "We should have followed her," I said.

Beattie didn't even dignify that idea with an eyeroll and instead simply went into the bathroom and closed the door. When I heard the shower start, I knew she was taking one of what she called her "shut out the world" showers, and I was fairly sure that I and my desire for adventure were part of the world she wanted to shut out.

A half-hour later, a cloud of steam escaped from the bathroom, and Beattie came out in a robe with a towel on her head. She had some sort of facial mask, and she was carrying a full kit of beauty supplies. "I left your mask on the sink. Open your pores first, and then we're doing a full regimen."

"Um, all right," I said. "Are you okay?"

"I am, and you're going to be okay, too. We just need a quiet night, so I'll get room service and cancel our reservation. We'll do our nails and such, and then we'll fall asleep to some British murder mystery. Sound okay?"

Something shifted in me, and I realized just how exhausted and overwhelmed I was by the international travel, the complications in our buying mission, and now the murder of Davis MacDonald. "Sounds perfect."

I stepped into the still-warm bathroom and turned the shower on as hot as I could stand. Beattie had not only put a clay mask on the side of the tub; she had also left her expensive bath wash for me to use with a brand new, natural loofah. That woman was pampering me, and I needed it.

I savored my shower and let the hot water soften up the muscles I hadn't even realized had tensed into tight knots. Then, I turned off the water, put on my mask, slipped into the robe on the back of the door and stepped out into the room. . . only to find Inspector Scott standing at the foot of my bed.

4

There's not much more awkward than greeting a police officer in your hotel room while only wearing a robe and a hot pink clay mask, but no one ever said my life wasn't awkward. I tried to make the best of the situation and put out my hand to say, "Nice to see you again, Inspector." The only problem was that my mask had begun to harden already, so what I said sounded more like, "Knife to ffuf ooh aga, Insector."

I'm sure my faced turned the same color as the mask, and for that reason alone, I was glad to be wearing it.

"Good to see you, too, Ms. Baxter. I was just telling Ms. Andrews here that I very much appreciated her call about your encounter with Ms. MacDonald." The inspector pointed to the only chair in the room by the desk. "May I sit?"

Beattie, who had somehow removed her mask and put on her very presentable plaid pjs, said, "Of course," and perched on the edge of the bed.

I decided to follow suit but promptly toppled over on the bed, saving my dignity by grabbing my robe as I teetered on the edge before falling to the floor. The night was just getting better and better.

When I had righted myself on the bed and draped the spare blanket over my lap so I could sit cross-legged without flashing anyone, the inspector continued. "As I was saying, thank you for calling about your conversation with Ms. MacDonald. She has been, well, a bit intrusive about the investigation."

Without thinking I said, "Well, it is her dad."

Beattie shot me a look that mirrored the ones my teachers used to give me when I used to dominate the conversation in class.

The inspector stared at me for a minute, and then said, "Actually, Davis was not her father but her great-uncle. He had provided for her for years, but despite his best efforts to be discreet, it was apparent that his niece did not truly value his support." He shook his head.

I studied the inspector in front of me. "You and Mr. MacDonald were friends?" It was the only I figured he would know such personal information.

"Aye," he said. "For over forty years, ever since grade school. That woman had no idea what her uncle gave up for her." He hung his head.

This time, it was Beattie that got nosy. "What do you mean?"

The inspector looked up slowly. "Davis MacDonald was a man of some means, and he gladly shared his wealth with anyone in need. But he also needed a great deal of time alone, a luxury that he was careful to guard tightly."

"Except when his niece was concerned," I said quietly.

"Precisely, Lass. Ms. MacDonald insisted on having weekly writing salons of some sort in his living room, and often these gatherings would last late into the night with some of the guests staying over. Sometimes for days at a time." The inspector shook his head.

"She fancied herself some sort of Scottish Hemingway, it sounds like," I said as I thought about the group of literary elites that Hemingway had known during the years he lived in Paris.

The inspector guffawed. "She did," he said with a long chuckle.

"The question is, though, did they wear berets?" I don't know quite why it felt appropriate to joke with this police officer, but it did. He laughed, the mood lightened, and I almost forgot I was in a robe and looking a bit like I'd gotten the world's worst sunburn.

"But her uncle didn't put a stop to the parties?" Beattie asked after she finished giggling herself. "He didn't change the locks."

"Oh no, never," the inspector said. "He would never have done that. I suggested that he simply suggest to her that he rent her a larger apartment so she could have the salons at her own place, but when he brought up that idea, she dismissed it because she needed her own space to keep her 'creative energy clear.'"

This time, I rolled my eyes. I didn't discount that creativity required space and maybe even clear energy, but the fact that this woman couldn't see the hypocrisy in her own words galled me. "Do you think she had something to do with his murder?" I asked.

The inspector rubbed a hand over his mustache. "If you hadn't called to tell me about her conversation with you, I wouldn't have even considered the possibility, but now, I must. From what you described, Ms. Andrews, I have to concur that she was trying to get information and perhaps about this book that you were seeking."

I nodded. "Beattie told you that we didn't give her much information."

"That was wise," he said. "But I wonder if I can get your help with a little something in that regard."

Beattie and I looked at each other, exchanged a silent agreement, and then Beattie said, "Sure, Inspector. How can we help?"

"I need the name of the man to whom Davis sold this book of sea monster stories." He looked from her to me and then back again.

"Seamus Stovall," I said as the Inspector's eyes came back my way. "He lives in Edinburgh."

"Very good," he said as he stood. "You leave for the Highlands in the morning, you say? Might I take the liberty of booking you a room at a friend's bed and breakfast near Loch Ness for tomorrow night?"

"That would be wonderful," I said and saw Beattie smiling too. "Thank you."

"I'll text you the address, and thank you for your cooperation." The inspector gave a small wave and walked out the door.

I knew there was a lot we could talk about from the inspector's visit, but I wasn't up to it tonight. Instead, I took the bottle of purple nail polish and said, "May I give you a pedicure?"

"Of course," Beattie said in a terrible English accent. "But only if I may return the favor?"

We spent the rest of the night watching Hamish MacBeth and trying out various polish colors on each other. By the time we drifted off in the middle of an episode, our toes were dry, and I had all but forgotten about Davis MacDonald.

5

A t 6 a.m. when Beattie's alarm, for some ungodly reason, went off, I woke with a start and all the events of the previous few days came rushing back. The break last night had been amazing, but now I had to contend with reality. I was just glad that reality was going to include deep lochs, mountains, and a castle or two.

Breakfast was, as usual, quite filling, and we ate until we were stuffed and then headed south. As promised, Inspector Scott had made arrangements as his friends' B&B, and so as soon as we reached the area around Loch Ness, we greeted the charming couple who was hosting us, dropped off our bags, and headed immediately to the water to see if we could catch a glimpse of the old girl herself.

Unfortunately, Nessie decided to stay in the deeps, but we did enjoy studying all the purported photos of her at the local museum in Drumnadrochit. I even climbed up on a giant sculpture of Nessie and had Beattie take my picture giving her a kiss. We then spent the rest of the afternoon wandering the back roads and taking short hikes with BB around the loch. The landscape was gorgeous with rocky hills and vistas everywhere, and by the time we headed back to our room we were both filled up with natural bliss.

Our hosts recommended a little pub just down in Fort Augustus at the South End of the lake, and we headed down and found, to our delight, a sprawling castle-like fort with a waterfront restaurant called The Boathouse. I had the Scottish version of macaroni and cheese, which was rich and hearty, and Beattie tried the prawns in cream sauce. Both of us were stuffed by the end of the meal and loved that the staff invited us to stay as long as we'd like and then to try dessert.

The evening was chilly but perfect, and I tucked my sweater around me and sipped my tea while looking out over the water. I would have been content to sit there well past dark, but then I caught a glimpse of someone who looked familiar down on the docks below the restaurant.

I jabbed Beattie in the arm with my finger and said, "Isn't that Seamus Stovall?" The man was stepping out of a sailboat in a full-on sailing outfit with a blue blazer, white cap, and khakis. If he hadn't carried himself with such seriousness, he would have looked absurd. Instead, he looked arrogant beyond measure.

"Well, I'll be," Beattie said. "What is he doing here, do you think?"

I shook my head. "No idea, but maybe we should let Inspector Scott know?"

"Good idea." Beattie took out her phone and typed in a quick text.

His reply was almost instantaneous, and she read it to me. "Oh good, he took the bait."

"The bait? What bait? What's going on?" I heard a shrill edge sneaking into my voice and tried to calm myself, but I could sense something was building. And I didn't like it. Not a bit, and especially not on my vacation.

Beattie was already typing, and a moment later her phone

rang. Since we were the only people on this part of the deck, she answered the call at the table. "Inspector. Thank you for calling. Please tell us what's going on." She held the phone away from her ear, so I could lean over and hear him too.

"I should have told you my plan, lasses. I am sorry. But I've set up a bit of a meeting with Stovall, Ms. MacDonald, and me there in Drumnadochit," the inspector said.

"A meeting?" I asked, "about Davis?"

"Well, ostensibly about his estate. I've told both of them that there are some questions about his book collection and I could use their help sorting through things." The inspector took a deep breath. "I was actually going to call on you in the morning to see if the two of you might act as appraisers of a sort."

I looked over at Beattie, and she scowled. "Act as appraisers, or actually be appraisers?"

"That's a good question. Both, maybe. I've told them I have experts coming in to value the book collection, and I'd actually like you all to do that. But I'd also like you to help me suss out how this book you're seeking to buy might play into the situation." He cleared his throat. "It seems this curse had more validity than I had first understood."

I grinned. "So are you saying you believe in the curse now, Inspector?"

He laughed. "No, no I am not, Ms. Beattie. I am saying that other people do, namely Davis, Stovall, and Ms. MacDonald, and I'd like your observations about the book and their reactions to it to see if they shed any light on Davis's death."

I nodded before I registered that he couldn't see me. "We can do that," I said without looking at Beattie, who was violently shaking her head. "When do you need us, and where?"

"Thank you, lasses," he said. "Does 2 p.m. at the Fiddlers' Highland suit you? I'll be buying everyone lunch."

"You'd better," Beattie said under her breath.

"Suits us fine, Inspector. See you then." She started to press the button to hang up but then she thought of something. "Did you ask Stovall to bring the book?"

"Of course, Ms. Beattie. Of course I did. See you tomorrow."

She hung up, and she and I squared off over our newly filled cups of tea and the plate of shortbread the waitress has brought us. "I cannot believe you agreed to this," she said.

To buy myself a moment, I shoved a whole piece of shortbread in my mouth and took my time chewing. Finally, I said, "Aren't you the least bit curious about what happened?"

She shook her head. "Not curious enough to get myself involved in a murder investigation."

"We're already involved, Beattie," I said gently. "We were involved even before we found MacDonald's body. If that book is part of the story, then we are not just involved; we're at the heart of things."

She took a second to think about that and then nodded. "You're right, but we don't have to be even more involved."

I tilted my head. "Not even if it means we get more information about the book and maybe another great story for its provenance?"

When a little glow came into her cheeks, I knew I had her. My best friend was a sucker for a story, especially if it added to the value of a book. But she didn't grant me the satisfaction of saying I was right. Instead, she just picked up her own piece of shortbread, took a small bite, and smiled out at the loch.

THE NEXT DAY, we dedicated our morning to simple sightseeing. First, we visited the beautiful Falls of Divach and then came back to the loch to visit the sixteenth century Urquhart Castle. We spent hours wandering the battlements and then sitting quietly overlooking the loch. I had a very hard time imagining anything but a sort of Disney-esque version of castle life, but somehow the life-size trebuchet wasn't making me feel warm and cozy. It was pretty terrifying actually.

But the waterfall and the castle had the wonderful effect of soothing my nerves, and even Beattie, who was still quite hesitant about our afternoon plans, seemed more light-hearted by the time we headed back into town and the Fiddler's Rest.

Still, when we walked up the street from where we'd parked our rental car, my heart started to pound at the sight of the Inspector and Ms. MacDonald at an outdoor table. I usually wasn't much of a beer drinker, but I was grateful to also see a pitcher of something golden and bubbly on the table. A little alcohol might make the afternoon smoother for me, and I appreciated the European openness to daytime drinking a little more.

We took our seats after saying hello, and Beattie tried to make small talk with our companions while we waited for Stovall. Unfortunately, Ms. MacDonald seemed intent on scowling and huffing things under her breath the entire time, so the ten-minute wait for Stovall to arrive felt like it was more than an hour. I made it through half a beer in my nervousness and then almost chugged the rest of the glass when I saw Stovall walking up the street. What had I gotten us into?

Stovall took his seat and shook everyone's hands. Then, he said, "So what is this all about, Inspector? It was quite an inconvenience to come up from the city."

I thought of the sailboat and his fancy sailing outfit and highly doubted the veracity of his words, but I held my tongue and let the Inspector take the lead.

"Well, as I said on the phone, Mr. Stovall, Davis MacDonald has died, and I have reason to believe that the book you now have in your possession may have been part of the motivation for his murder." The inspector's voice was even and steady, unlike my heartrate.

Stovall frowned. "Why would you suspect that? I've owned the book for several months now, and Davis and I made an agreeable exchange on both sides."

I had to admit I was curious about how the inspector was going to answer this question without saying something like, "Well, Ms. MacDonald here seems suspiciously interested in the book," which was the only thing I could think of.

But to his credit, the inspector only said, "I cannot reveal details about the investigation, but I can say that we have significant evidence to suggest that someone might have killed Mr. MacDonald to obtain that book."

"But he didn't even have the book," Ms. MacDonald shrieked. "I looked and looked for it—" She abruptly stopped talking as she realized she had said far too much in just those few words.

"Why were you looking for the book?" This time Beattie had stepped in to ask a question.

I looked over at the inspector, but he seemed completely unaffected by her intervention.

Ms. MacDonald, however, had turned a sort of greenish-pink and looked like she might have swallowed a bee. "Well, simply," she sputtered, "I knew the book was valuable and wanted to be sure it was safe."

"When did you look for the book?" the inspector asked.

This question made Ms. MacDonald visibly squirm in her seat, and I could almost see her brain trying to work out what answer would get her in to the least trouble. After a few moments, her shoulders sagged, and she said, "Two nights ago, after he was killed."

That sounded like the truth if I'd ever heard it, and if that was true, then it might have been motivation enough for Ms. MacDonald to kill him, especially if she thought he still had the book and didn't think he'd give it to her if he was alive.

"Why did you want to find the book?" I asked, perfectly aware that she had already offered one reason for her search.

She glared at me. "Like I said, I wanted to be sure the book was safe and secure."

I sighed. So much for my hope that she'd slip up and give another reason. Still, despite her consistency, I didn't quite believe her. That said, she might have just wanted the book out of greed after the fact but might not have had the gumption to commit murder to get it.

The inspector took control of the conversation again. "Stovall, tell us the details of your transaction with Davis MacDonald." This time, he was more forceful, less placating, and I knew we were getting to the meat of the conversation now.

"I'd prefer not to talk about the money, if you don't mind," Stovall said with a casualness that felt overly confident given that a man had been murdered. Plus, he'd already told us what he paid. It seemed odd to withhold that information from the police.

"I do mind," the inspector said. "All the details please."

For a split second, I saw anger on Stovall's face, but then he slid his mask of studied casualness back into place. "Very well then. I paid Davis MacDonald 25,000 pounds for the book."

I sighed. At least he had been truthful, and Beattie and I didn't have to correct him. Still, it was curious he hadn't wanted to share that information.

"And was that fair market value?" The inspector asked.

Next to him, Ms. MacDonald was turning a very, very deep shade of red, but she was holding her tongue. I decided to follow her lead, although I wasn't sure why.

Stovall took a deep breath and stared out beyond me into the street. His silence grew so long that I began to feel antsy, but eventually he said, "Fair market value is whatever someone will pay or sell for. That's how capitalism works."

The inspector sighed and then looked at Beattie and then me. "Is that fair market value?"

Beattie didn't hesitate. "No, the book is worth at least a third to two-thirds more than that."

"Maybe twice that if more of the provenance can be proven," I added and was pleased to see Beattie nod. I was getting the hang of this book buying business, I supposed.

"I knew it," Ms. MacDonald shouted. "I knew you swindled my uncle. I'd like my book back please." She actually held out her hand like Stovall was just going to place the book in it.

The inspector shook his head. "Mr. Stovall, I presume you have a formal bill of sale."

"Of course," Stovall said as he reached into his bag and pulled out a stapled set of papers that I presumed was identical to the one he had given us. He handed the papers to the inspector and then looked over at me. "Perhaps we should discuss your offer again over dinner?"

I gave him a brisk nod because, after all, my job here was to buy the book, but I knew Beattie and I would be making a plan before we spent any more time with that man.

"Excuse me," Ms. MacDonald said. "That book is my property. I am my, um," she glanced at Beattie and I, "my uncle's sole heir."

"Your uncle?" Beattie said with a feigned shock that even involved her hand flying to her mouth.

Ms. MacDonald shrugged. "Fathers are more dear, I figured." Then she looked at the inspector. "That book belongs to me. This man tricked my uncle into selling it for far less than it's worth. That has to be a crime that nullifies the sale."

Stovall didn't even bat an eye, probably because he knew, as the rest of us did, that Ms. MacDonald was making a ridiculous claim.

"I'm afraid, Ms. MacDonald, that your uncle signed a legal

bill of sale and so the book rightfully belongs to Mr. Stovall."
He sighed. "Additionally, you are not your uncle's heir."

I thought, perhaps, Ms. MacDonald was going to pass out
or burst a blood vessel from fury because she sputtered and spit
as she tried to respond to the inspector. Finally, she blurted,
"You're full of nonsense, Inspector Scott. My attorney will be in
touch." Then she stood up, poured her beer on Stovall's head
and stormed off.

I had to give her credit for a dramatic entrance, and I
couldn't say I didn't take a little pleasure from seeing Stovall
drenched in ale. But her reasons for being upset were so ridiculous that I had to suppress a laugh at her ire.

Beattie, however, had no such desire for tact and broke into
laughter as soon as Ms. MacDonald was a few feet away. The
inspector gave her a big grin, and Stovall, even though he was
soaked, seemed to take the moment in stride as he wiped
himself down with a monogrammed handkerchief. "She does
seem a wee bit upset," he said as he patted his khakis dry.

"A bit," I said as I began to giggle, too. "Her sense of entitle-
ment is quite profound," I managed to say between laughs.

The inspector nodded. "Indeed. She has no claim to the
book or her uncle's estate, however. He left everything to a cat
charity."

This news broke Beattie and me out in laughter again,
despite the scowl BB gave me from where he sat in his bag
under the table. Butterball was not, obviously, a fan of cats.

Finally, Beattie and I managed to get ourselves under
control, and the inspector returned to the purpose of our meeting. "Mr. Stovall, do you know of anyone else who was interested in acquiring this book?" He looked down at Stovall's
briefcase where, presumably, he had the book.

Stovall didn't hesitate this time. "Besides the Library of
Scotland, no." He stated this fact simply and without any
reproach. "They simply decided to pass on the sale, which took

away any leverage Davis had in obtaining a better price. I presumed he needed the money, which was why he was selling in the first place. I did nothing untoward. It was simply business."

In my experience, people often used the phrase "it was simply business" to alleviate some deeply ignored guilt they had about taking advantage of someone else, but he wasn't wrong about the nature of the transaction. Davis had agreed, and so that was that.

I felt like we had gone as far as we could in this discussion and looked over to Beattie to see if she might be ready to leave. When I saw her face, though, I settled back into my seat. She was thinking about something, something worrying, and when her face was still and fixed like a statue, I knew better than to try to move her.

I also knew that she needed a moment to gather her thoughts, so I tried to keep the men talking. "So do you think Ms. MacDonald just assumed that her uncle had left everything to her, or might he have led her to believe he had?"

The inspector shook his head. "Davis would never have given her that impression." He frowned. "But he might not have had the vim to dissuade her of it either."

"Given her reaction today, I can see why," I said as I looked over at Beattie again. This time, she was looking at me.

"I think we may need to invite someone to our little gathering here," she said with a bit of sadness as she stared at me. "Adaire."

I stared back at my friend and realized she was right just as my own pinch of sadness reached my chest. "Oh yeah, that would be good, I guess." My voice wasn't very convincing.

"Who's Adaire?" The inspector asked.

"He's the librarian that we've been working with," Beattie spoke quietly. "He's actually in Inverness right now."

"Or at least he was when we left," I said, hoping beyond

hope that he had actually gone back to Edinburgh early the day after we had dinner. Our date wasn't scheduled until tomorrow night, though, so I thought the chances that he was still in the area were pretty good. "I can text him," I said reluctantly.

"Please do," the inspector said. "We will all meet for lunch in Inverness tomorrow. Same time." This wasn't a request, and despite the hard look on Stovall's face, I saw he didn't object. I couldn't say I expected Ms. MacDonald to do the same.

It took some restraint on my part, after we left the pub, to not try to explain the whole situation to Adaire via text, but given that we hadn't spoken since two days before, I decided a long text with all the details of the past day's events was a little bit of overload in general and probably unwise when it came to solving MacDonald's murder. So I went with, "You still in Inverness by chance?"

His reply was quick. "Coming back tomorrow morning before our date. Why?"

I couldn't help feeling the flush at his use of the word "date." My excitement quickly faded, though, as I tried to figure out what to say about needing to meet him for lunch. I didn't want him getting the wrong impression, but I couldn't bring myself to type, "I need you to meet with a police officer about a murder."

Instead, I typed, "I'd like you to meet some folks. Up for lunch with Beattie, some acquaintances, and me tomorrow at 2?"

"Sure. I'd love to meet your friends." He even included a smiley emoji.

Again, I was stymied about how to clarify, so I just wrote, "Great" and sent back my own smiley. Then I groaned.

Beattie looked over at me from the large cinnamon roll she'd just bought. Like me, she ate when she was on edge, and I had to admit that bun looked delicious, almost as good as one

I'd once had in a bookstore café in a Maryland town. "Not good news?" she asked.

I shrugged. "He's coming, but I'm not sure if that's good news or not. I feel like I just set him up for an ambush."

"If he's the murderer, Poe, then he deserves to be ambushed." Her words were true, but her eyes were soft.

"And if he's not?"

6

Since Beattie and I weren't going to be able to get further into the Highlands after all, we decided we'd at least drive out to Eilean Donan, as the inspector had suggested, before heading back to Inverness. We decided to go ahead and make the trip that afternoon so that we could watch the sunset over the castle as one of our guidebooks suggested.

The drive out was beautiful, and once again, I found myself feeling right at home and thought it might be worth my while to dig into my family genealogy a bit and see if I had Scottish roots. In every way, this landscape felt like coming home, partially, I knew, because it reminded me a bit of the rolling hills of Virginia but also because of a wildness that just felt right and good in my soul.

I hadn't traveled the world enough yet to know if I'd feel this same way in any rugged space, and maybe I would. But just then, I let myself sink into the space and imagine myself living here in the time of the clans, when the people of your clan were your family, your protection, and your government.

When we drove down the lane to the castle, I caught my breath. The building itself was gorgeous, much smaller than

Urquhart but also more intact. Plus, it sat in the water on a small island and, thus, felt even more like a fortress. Plus, since we were in an even more remote part of the country, the place felt more peaceful as well as more exposed. I loved it instantly.

We bought tickets and apologized to the docent for our late arrival. He was a friendly man and said he always loved the last tour of the day, especially when it was personal like ours was. "You two lasses get my special stories," he said with a wink, and I squeezed Beattie's arm. This was going to be a great treat.

For the next two hours, our guide gave us a story-rich tour of the castle, every room and window, every horror story from both life and afterlife sources. It was amazing, and I wished it would go on forever.

But alas, we finally wound our way back to the giftshop and began to saw our goodbyes. I was just about to ask if I could get our guide's address so I could send him a little note of thanks when I suddenly realized I might be talking to a resident sea monster expert since the castle sits near where three sea-formed lochs meet. "Dudley," I asked, referring to him by the name he'd asked us to use, "do you know anything about sea monsters here?"

If Dudley hadn't regaled us with at least a dozen ghost stories about the area, I might have been hesitant to ask such a touristy question, but given the enthusiasm he had used in telling his stories, I figured he might just enjoy the chance to tell one or two more.

He turned to face me head-on and said, "Oh yes, Nessie isn't our only serpent, you know?" Then he winked. "We have all kinds of tales, but mostly from up north. Why do you ask, lass?"

I was getting very much used to being called lass, and I thought about asking Beattie to call me that too from now on. "Well, we are here on a work trip actually, a trip to buy a famous book about sea monsters. So I'm just asking everyone for stories." It wasn't exactly a lie, even if it wasn't quite the full truth.

I was surprised when Dudley's face grew very stern. "You're not looking to purchase the Sea Monster Chronicles, are you, lass? If you are, I must caution you against such a foolhardy thing." He leaned in closer to us and lowered his voice. "That book is cursed."

I stared at Dudley for a moment, waiting for him to wink again, but his face stayed hard and he shook his head. "Steer clear if you value your lives," he said and then shook our hands quickly and disappeared into a back room.

Until a few moments before, I had been hoping to make it worthwhile for the shop attendant to stay open for us by picking up some souvenirs and gifts for folks at home, but Dudley's caution had made me eager to get on the road so Beattie and I could talk. Still, I picked up a couple of books about the castle and a goofy-looking ball cap for Uncle Fitz before we headed out and watched from the car as the lights went out inside the castle.

THE TWO-HOUR DRIVE back to Inverness was mostly quiet except for the few times Beattie and I decided to try and puzzle out why people would think this book was cursed. Clearly, there were many tragic things associated with the tome, but so far, it seemed like most of those, at least in relation to our desire to purchase it, were related to financial greed. Neither of us could figure out the kind of folklore that would lead people to believe that a book of old tales about monsters from the water would lead people to believe it caused the death of people on land.

It was only when we came back into Inverness and crossed two bridges before getting to our hotel that I realized just how very much water was in this part of Scotland. As I pondered this fact while eating the takeaway Indian food that we'd picked up next to the hotel, I tried to think about other legends involving water. Selkies and mermaids, naiads and nixies. Most cultures had a water spirit or monster of some sort.

As Beattie settled into bed with her book, I opened my laptop and searched for folktales about water creatures here in Scotland. I quickly found the various sea monster legends that were compiled in the book we were seeking to buy, but it was the legends of the Kelpies and the Ashrays that kept me reading well into the night. Kelpies were water creatures who took the shape of horses and led humans to their deaths while Ashrays were ghost-like creatures who lived in deep water and only came out at night.

According to legend, Ashrays had far more reason to be afraid of humans than us of them since if touched by any sunlight at all, they'd dissolve into a pool of water. The worst they seemed to be able to do to humans was leave a permanent cold spot anywhere they touched us.

Kelpies, however, sounded a bit like horse-shaped sirens, and despite the more modern depictions that often showed sirens as beautiful and oft-misunderstood maidens, the actual stories were of evil women who showed no hesitation or remorse about luring sailors to their deaths. The same seemed to be true of kelpies, except that their trick was to appear as tame, beautiful horses who, if you mounted them, would not let you off and would then drag you to your death in a nearby stream or river.

What was interesting to me is that both these legends were about freshwater creatures, a fact that haunted my dreams long after I finally closed the computer and went to sleep. I kept seeing Davis MacDonald being dragged into the Inverness River by a horse, or a young woman dissolving into a puddle a la the Wicked Witch in The Wizard of Oz.

When Beattie's alarm woke me at 7, I felt more tired than

when I'd gone to sleep, and I had this nagging sensation that my subconscious had been trying to show me something through all those dreams. But as was usual with my dreams, I couldn't draw anything coherent from them once I was awake.

I went down to breakfast feeling groggy but agitated, and even the sizable portions of Belgian waffles available in the breakfast room didn't lift my spirits. I just couldn't shake the sensation that I was missing something, something really important.

Given that I didn't really know how to explain my thinking to Beattie, I decided to force my questions out of my head and enjoy the morning. We were going to do a whirlwind tour of all Inverness had to offer, starting with the art museum. Then, we were going to take in the castle and finally have a snack at the botanical gardens before our meeting.

Between the beauty, the heavy walking, and the number of snacks we decided to grab as we walked, the morning flew by, and I thought nary a bit about the book, the curse, or the gathering that afternoon. But when we stopped by the hotel to grab BB so he could come along for an outing as well as a potential escape excuse if we needed one, my nerves charged ahead.

We were going to be meeting with three people who, I was fairly sure, Inspector Scott considered murder suspects. While I didn't really want to break bread with anyone who might have killed another person, it was sitting at the table with Adaire that was making me the most anxious. I liked the guy, that was no secret, and so I really hoped he wasn't a murderer.

But what was more disconcerting to me was that I might have really misjudged someone. I didn't know what to make of the fact that I might have a crush on someone who could kill or that my judgment might be that off. Just the idea of it was throwing my whole sense of self into a bit of a tizzy.

Still, I forced myself to take some deep breaths, snuggle Butterball close while we were in the hotel, and then concentrate on the beautiful waterside view when we got to the small restaurant the inspector had chosen. We were the first to arrive after the officer himself, so when we sat down, he took a few minutes to play with BB through his translucent bag, and when I gave him permission, he slipped BB a couple of chips, which the hamster gobbled up as if he had not been fed five minutes earlier.

Adaire arrived next, and he gave me a kiss on the cheek before scooting a chair right next to mine and sitting down. He greeted Beattie warmly and then extended a hand to the inspector, who shook it while shooting me a very raised eyebrow. Maybe I should have told him that I had a date with Adaire that night.

The inspector took a few moments to ask Adaire about himself, and when he learned the librarian had grown up in Inverness, they exchanged a few names of people they might have in common. It turned out that Adaire's parents were good friends with the inspector's sister, and while that connection seemed to relax the two men, it made me more on edge because now even more was at stake.

Fortunately, when Stovall and then Ms. MacDonald arrived in short order, the focus switched entirely to the murder of Davis MacDonald, a fact that Adaire had heard about but hadn't realized was related to the book. "You think someone killed him to get the book?" Adaire asked.

The inspector shook his head. "I don't know the motive at all at this point, but it seems possible given how famous and in high demand the book is." His voice was quieter today, and I couldn't tell if that was because he was a little less sure of his theory or because he was downplaying the situation in the hopes that someone would open up and talk.

It also occurred to me that I had not yet heard the inspector offer any other explanation for Davis MacDonald's murder, and as sure as I was that the book was involved, it suddenly seemed a little odd that the police inspector wasn't considering other, more obvious possibilities like robbery or bad blood with someone MacDonald knew. So, true to form, I showed absolutely no tact and asked, "Couldn't someone have just been mad at MacDonald and killed him? Or maybe someone wanted to rob his house? It sounds like he had lots of valuables there, from what you've said." My own voice grew quiet at the end of my query as I realized that I may have just sounded a bit defensive rather than simply curious.

The inspector looked at me and nodded. "Those are definitely possibilities, Ms. Baxter, and I assure you I am looking into them all. Thus far, however, nothing seems to be panning out in that regard. Nothing was missing from the house, and no one admits to having a grudge against Davis." He cut his eyes toward Ms. MacDonald, but she didn't seem to notice. "So without more firm leads, I am following the most viable one, the Sea Monster Chronicles."

I sighed and nodded, trying to get the twinge of a question I could still feel in my throat to quiet down. I wasn't quite sure why I felt there was more to what was going on than I could say, but I figured it wouldn't do much good to say anything more about it. At least until I could talk to Beattie alone again.

"Now, tell me what you know of this curse," the inspector said to Adaire.

If Adaire was surprised by the question, he didn't show it. "Well, I know the legend is that anyone who owns the book drops dead, and I understand that the cause of death is usually somehow associated with water or a mirror."

Beattie nodded. "That's what we've heard, too. Was there water around MacDonald's body?"

I glanced quickly over at Beattie, but she gently tapped her foot against mine in the universal, "be quiet" signal. So she wasn't suddenly a believer in the curse, but she did have a theory. I couldn't wait to hear what it was.

Inspector Scott raised one eyebrow and looked at her but then said, "No. There was a large mirror in the room though." It was my turn to raise an eyebrow, and I wondered if Beattie had nudged him under the table, too.

Ms. MacDonald sucked in a quick breath, but by the time I looked at her, her face was stoic and staid . . . and looking right at me. "Surely you've heard the rumors about the curse," I asked as innocently as I could muster.

She sighed. "That's a bunch of malarkey," she spat. "Perpetuated by people who are not willing to move into the twenty-first century. Those legends were created to explain phenomena that people didn't understand, like cardiac arrest and electromagnetic impulses. They were created to dispel fear, not actually explain anything."

I stared at Ms. MacDonald a bit dumbfounded for a moment, because of course that was exactly why folklore was created: to explain the unexplainable. But there was something about how adamantly she was decrying the truth of the curse that made me suspicious. I wasn't sure why because she sounded, well, a lot like me. Still, something was up.

"True enough," I said, ceding her point but not being willing to pick up an argument I didn't actually have an investment in. "But I was reading last night about ashrays and kelpies. Are there stories about them being in the river here?"

Beattie looked at me out of the corner of her eye, but she didn't say anything.

Adaire nodded. "A few. Most of them are tales from outside the city, but the older ones, some of them have roots here." He shook his head. "But I have to agree that there's not validity to the legends."

"The question," the inspector said, "was did Davis believe in the curse?"

I looked over at the inspector. "Why does that matter?"

"Because if he did, someone may have taken advantage of

that fact," Beattie said with a steady nod of her head. "Had the mirror been hanging in the room long?"

All of us looked to Ms. MacDonald, but it was the inspector who spoke. "No, I had never seen it before."

Ms. MacDonald glanced at him sharply. "That's right. I assumed when I saw it that Uncle had just bought it." She looked down at her hands. "But maybe someone else placed it there to scare him."

Inspector Scott nodded. "That's what I suspect. From what I knew, Davis wasn't a particularly superstitious man, so I'm puzzled." He looked over at Ms. MacDonald.

"Don't look at me. I have no idea about any of this." She studied her intertwined fingers again. "Uncle and I weren't particularly close."

I wasn't sure what to make of that statement, so I asked another question. "Do you think he might have sold you the book at such a low price," I asked as I turned to Stovall, "because he was scared of the curse?"

Stovall reached down and pulled the blue book out of his briefcase and set it in the center of the table. "Honestly, I have no idea. He never mentioned a curse. Of course I knew about the stories before I approached him to purchase the book, but it never came up in our conversations."

"Did he seem nervous or anxious at all?" Beattie asked.

"Not that I noticed," Stovall said. "He was pleasant and professional, and while I was pleased to get the book at such a good price, he didn't seem ridiculously eager to let it go." He paused for a minute. "In fact, now that we're talking about it, I do remember thinking I didn't really understand his reason for selling. But honestly, motivation is none of my business when it comes to acquiring collectibles."

I studied Stovall for a minute, but I didn't note anything that made me think he was being anything but truthful. In fact, Uncle Fitz had told me often enough that the reason someone is selling is none of his business. He is there to make an exchange, not explore the story behind the exchange. "Keep it professional, Poe. That's the bottom line," he'd said.

It seemed Stovall and Uncle Fitz followed the same ethic, and I had to admit that at this point in my first buying adventure I would have been quite happy to not know the story behind this book and be heading to the Isle of Skye to relax with Beattie instead of trying to figure out a murder.

The previous night, I had blown off Stovall's invitation to discuss the sale of the book because I just wanted to get away with Beattie, but now, I was curious. "So is all this talk of the curse what made you more eager to sell?" I said with far less subtlety than I intended.

Stovall smirked at me. "No, my dear. But if it has made you more eager to buy, then we really must meet to discuss terms."

I rolled my eyes and glanced at Adaire, who was looking at me with a slight furrow between his eyebrows. I couldn't read his expression, but it didn't make me think he was happy at the moment.

"We will definitely discuss the book again, Mr. Stovall, but I think perhaps we will do that when we all return to Edinburgh. I have other plans for my final night here in Inverness." I wanted to be the kind of woman who would look over at her date and wink, but I wasn't that woman. So instead, I blushed and hoped Adaire caught my meaning, and that he was happy about it.

"One last question for everyone here, if I may," the inspector said, bringing us back to the point of our meeting. "What is, would you say, the actual value of the Sea Monster Chronicles? Can you come to a consensus on a figure?"

The looks that shot around the table reminded me of the way my family had studied each other over the Monopoly board at family reunions. We'd played tournament style, four players to a team, and with over 100 people on my dad's side, that meant we had a lot of Monopoly boards.

The competition was fierce, and the strategies varied. Some of us bought up anything and everything. Some of us went for the big value targets, and a few die-hards scooped up anything cheap and, often, creamed us all. By the time the last four players were left on the final board, the bets were flying and the competitors extremely focused.

For the past two years, I had been in that final four, and both times I had lost to my Great-Aunt Mildred, who somehow managed to keep the rules of Monopoly straight even though her mind had long ago led her to believe it was 1949. She wiped the floor with me, my cousin Sid, and my Uncle Earl, and she gloated. I wouldn't have been surprised to see her do one of those endzone dances when she finally took the game.

Now, though, the looks flying around the table were even more intense. Stovall was eyeing me like he dared me to say less than he was asking, and Beattie was looking at Adaire with what I can only call skepticism. Ms. MacDonald kept peering at each of us in turn as if she could see her inheritance on the tip of each of our tongues.

Eventually, I grew tired of the sizing-up process and said, "I value the book at no more than $40,000 US."

Beattie nodded. "$45K at best, if we can discover a bit more of the provenance."

Stovall scoffed. "The book is worth - at minimum - $50K US. That is the minimum I will take for it, not a –"

Inspector Scott interrupted Stovall and said, "I'm actually not at all interested in your business terms here, Mr. Stovall. I need to understand the value of the book in question, and Ms. Poe and Ms. Beattie have given me a range of $40-45K US. That is sufficient. Thank you."

The inspector could have asked us that question at any of the many times we'd been alone together, including just a bit ago when we arrived, but clearly, he had a motivation for asking with all of us gathered.

"If I may, I would say that the Library values the book at considerably more than either of those estimates, more in the range of $60-75K US," Adaire said quietly.

This time Beattie's contact with my leg was more of a kick-boxer's blow than a nudge, and I couldn't blame her. This figure was news to me, and apparently to everyone else at the table too judging by their expressions.

Even Inspector Scott seemed a little dumbfounded. "Please repeat that figure, sir."

"$60-75,000 US Dollars," Adaire said, louder this time, as if he was growing more confident with the figure. "The book is one of a kind, and given the place it has in the Scottish imagination, its value is considerable."

It was my turn to kick Beattie. What was all this about the place in the Scottish imagination? No one beyond a few book collectors and folklorists even knew the book existed. That didn't mean it wasn't valuable, but it wasn't exactly one of Elvis's sequin jumpsuits or whatever the Scottish equivalent would be. William Wallace's kilt?

Despite my skepticism about both Adaire's figure and his explanation for it, I kept my mouth shut. It seemed like a good time to follow the inspector's lead and let the conversation play out a bit.

And play out it did when Ms. MacDonald stood up and threw an arm so close to the inspector's face that her outstretched fingers almost grazed his nose. "I told you the book was valuable, very valuable, and you just acted like I was out of my mind."

The inspector cleared his throat and ignored her comment, even as she loomed over him as he continued to sit. "Would you be willing to write up that valuation officially?" he asked Adaire.

"Certainly," Adaire said. "I could get that to you in the morning if you'd like. I just have to get the letterhead file from the library, and then I can write it up officially for you."

"Very good," the inspector said as he stood and stepped to his right to avoid Ms. MacDonald. "In that case, I have everything I need for today. Mr. Stovall, I need to take the book at this point. If you'd like to go with me to the station, I can give you a formal receipt for it so that you can claim it again at the end of the investigation."

Stovall did not look pleased with this turn of events, but given that the inspector had already slid the book under his arm, the book dealer didn't have much of a choice but to nod and follow the inspector up the street, presumably to the station.

Ms. MacDonald lingered a few moments more as if she was still waiting for some sort of vindication, but then she moped off down the street in the opposite direction, leaving Beattie, Adaire, and me alone at the table.

"What was that?" I said to Adaire as soon as everyone else was out of earshot. "That value on the book is absurd." I sounded much more certain than I felt, given that this was my first purchasing trip, but I knew that Uncle Fitz wouldn't mislead me by $35,000 dollars.

"I agree," Adaire said without even a single ruffled and metaphorical feather. "But my bosses think that book has immense cultural value, and they're willing to pay top dollar." He smiled at me. "That should be good news for you because it will mean you'll make a larger profit, assuming you convince Stovall to sell."

"And how are we supposed to do that now that you've told him what the Library values the book for?" Beattie said with a shake of her head.

Adaire's face opened slowly into a wide smile. "Because I

am a man of my word, and I already agreed to buy the book from you," he glanced at me, "Or, rather, from Fitzhugh."

When Adaire looked at me and winked, I blushed. . . all the way down to my toes. I'm not exactly sure why. He was just making a business commitment, not telling me I was the most amazing woman he'd ever met. But somehow, I took it that way. I decided I was exhausted from all the investigation and took a long sip of my cider. That would definitely help.

Except it didn't help. Neither did the next two ciders or the two bags of crisps I ate as we hammered out a proposal to send, tentatively, to Uncle Fitz with our afternoon update about our progress. The cider and the crisps did, however, keep me from staring quite so hard at Adaire when he let his knee fall against mine under the table.

BY THE TIME Beattie finally decided it was time for us to head back to the hotel to send that email, I was pretty tipsy and also very thirsty because of the crisps, and I was absolutely in no shape to make any decision of any kind. I was barely in shape to stand up from the table safely, but I did manage that feat and acted like I was just being cute when I clutched onto Beattie's arm for the walk up the street to our hotel.

There is a massive difference between being cute and staying upright, but I didn't need Adaire to note that my purpose was the latter. In fact, I wasn't completely sure I wanted Adaire to note anything more about me because, given that his interest in me had been confirmed (unless his leg had fallen asleep or something), I was now freaking out completely. This was par for the course in dating for me.

As soon as we got to our room, Beattie ordered a large pot of Earl Grey tea, a plate of scones, and a cup of coffee. Then, she forced me to sit down, put my feet up, and let her give me a leg massage until I could breathe more easily. Once I had some caffeine in my system and was on my first mug of tea, she said, "Okay, what happened? Clearly, I missed something."

"He touched me," I said, and when my best friend's eyes narrowed in confusion, I said, "Maybe. His knee rested against mine under the table."

"So he did touch you then," she said matter-of-factly. "That's not in question. The question is whether that touch was intentional or not, correct?"

I nodded and felt my heart rate speed up again. Beattie gently lifted the mug of tea to my lips, and I took a long sip of creamy sweetness. "Okay, so what do you think?"

Beattie leaned back on the bed beside me and smiled. "Oh, he likes you." Then, she immediately pushed the mug up toward my mouth again, preempting my next panic. "I didn't even need the knee info to know that."

"But he knows I live in America, right?" I lifted the mug of my own accord this time.

"I presume so, but tonight we can make that very clear. The question you need to consider is what to do if he knows and doesn't care." She waggled her eyebrows.

I groaned. "Maybe we can just concentrate on making it through dinner." I sat bolt upright. "Oh no. What am I going to wear to dinner?"

As if I had suggested that bacon crisps were not delicious, Beattie scoffed. "Already handled." Then, she stood up, walked to the closet by the hotel door, opened it, and pulled out the only dress I'd brought – a maxi dress in navy blue.

I started to shake my head in protest to say that was going to be too chilly for tonight since it was sleeveless when Beattie put up a single finger and pulled an orange cardigan out from the closet.

"Before you say anything, no one here thinks of these as UVA colors, so you don't need to worry that you're betraying your principles or something," she said.

There was much I loved about our home city's school, the University of Virginia. The libraries, the beautiful buildings, the museums... but the culture of the place was a little too Old Virginia for me. Nostalgia with a sweater tied around its shoulders. I had purposefully chosen to go to William and Mary, an equally strong educational institution (not to mention the oldest in Virginia) but one with a lot less staked on its preppy reputation and football team. I *never* wore blue and orange together, though, because they were UVA colors, and I wasn't about to start now, even an ocean away.

"Sorry, Beats, no can do. I just can't stand the combo. Modify, please!" I waved my hand and lifted my pinky from the handle of my tea mug. "I know you have another option."

My best friend rolled her eyes, but then she immediately put back the orange sweater, pulled out a pink one of hers, and said, "Better?"

Twenty years ago, you would never have caught me in hot pink like this, but in the past couple of years, I'd begun to grow fond of bright colors – purple, bright blue, teal, and even orange when not paired with the university's navy. I chalked it up to becoming more comfortable with myself and not feeling like I needed to fade into the nature around me anymore.

"Better," I said and stood up. "Shoes?" I said as I began to undress so I could grab a quick shower. I was glad to find that I wasn't as prone to a leftward lean as before.

Beattie handed me a pair of platform shoes with ballet straps that ran up the ankles. "These would be perfect."

I looked at my own feet, several sizes smaller than hers, and said "They are adorable, but I will be clomping around in these. What else?"

She smiled at me and said, "We could shove tissue in the toes."

I looked down at the peep-toe shoes in beautiful pink leather. "Are you serious?"

"Fine," she said as she carefully set the shoes back in the bottom of the closet and took out my pair of black sandals. "Your feet will probably be cold, though." She made it sound like we were going to the arctic.

"Better cold than in shoes that don't fit me," I said as I headed to the shower.

"Says who?" she quipped after I shut the door.

I READ SOMEWHERE ONCE that the shower is the place most people get their best ideas, and one of the ideas I'd had after hearing that and thinking about it in the shower was that someone – not me – needed to invent a waterproof white board for just such shower musings. In fact, I needed one at that moment because as I mused about the events of the past few days while the very hot water beat against the back of my neck and shoulders, I suddenly had an idea.

Given, it wasn't that brilliant of an idea. In fact, I had slid past this very idea several times in our conversations in the past few days, but for some reason, I hadn't ever let my focus land squarely on it. Now, though, now that I'd settled on this possibility, it felt almost certain, like I had just figured out the keyword for the world's hardest cipher.

Beattie, however, did not seem to grasp the full depth of my insight when I said, "What if Davis MacDonald's murder wasn't about the book after all?" In fact, I think it's highly possible she rolled her eyes when she looked away from me to pick up the TV remote and change the channel. "What if?" she said with a level of apathy that would have been the envy of disaffected teenagers everywhere.

"So you've thought of this?" I said as I flopped over on the bed. "It's that obvious?"

She turned off the TV and turned to me. "Not necessarily.

After all, the inspector clearly thinks the book is the key, and he's the expert."

Just as I started to feel a little better, she continued, "But yeah, I did think of it earlier today when the conversation settled so soundly on the idea that the book was the motive."

I nodded and then smiled. "Ever the devil's advocate," I said.

"You know me?" she said with a wink as she went in to take her own shower.

As college students, we roommates had made it a point of eating meals together in our apartment at least four nights a week. It was a habit we'd all had with our families, and somehow, we fell into it as we ourselves became a family of choice.

At those dinners, Beattie had tried to stir up trouble by taking the opposite position on anything anyone else said. At the time, I found it completely annoying, as did the other three women, but we also knew it was just Beattie, keeping herself entertained and her super-charged brain engaged. At this moment, she was doing the same.

Except this time it didn't feel like Beattie was just creating a thought exercise. Something about the idea that there might be another motive for MacDonald's death rang true in a deep way for me. But as was common with me, my intuition was far ahead of my intellect. In that way, Beattie and I were opposites, a fact that made us a good team for most things, especially trivia nights at our local bars back home.

As I dressed, I mulled over possible alternative motives to keep myself distracted from the fact that I had a date with a guy I liked and who, apparently, liked me, but maybe only because I lived an ocean away. In the mystery books and detective shows, the motives for murder are always love, money, or revenge. Obviously, the book was related to money, especially if Adaire was correct about its full value, but I wondered if there might be other ways money could be involved. What was Davis MacDonald's net worth, I wondered.

In terms of love, I hadn't gotten any inkling that MacDonald was involved with anyone. In the limited view I'd gotten of his house when I'd stepped inside, I hadn't seen any photos of him with another person much less in a cuddling selfie or portrait that might say he was involved. Of course, that didn't mean he wasn't dating someone or hadn't dated someone in the past, but I needed more information to assess that possibility.

That left me with revenge. I was inclined to dismiss this option out of hand given how much of a pushover MacDonald had been with this great-niece and how glowing the inspector's words about him had been, I knew that that desire for revenge didn't necessarily warrant that MacDonald had done something awful.

Once, I'd had a neighbor who had sat in her car honking her horn at me for forty-five minutes after I blocked our shared driveway with my car when it had been rear-ended and slammed into a telephone pole. The car was unmovable, and the person in the vehicle behind me was injured. And yet, because my neighbor had a softball game she wanted to get to, she honked the entire time it took for the state troopers to arrive, assess the situation, and give her a stern warning about disturbing the peace.

From then on, she'd done everything in her power to make me miserable, including insisting that I not mow the area around our driveway because it was her property and my mower was "ruining her grass." Instead, she let it grow up to hay-height, making it almost impossible to see to turn out onto the road.

Fortunately, karma often takes things into her own hands, and one night when that neighbor was checking her mail, a huge black snake crawled out of that tall grass and across her feet. She mowed the next day. It was beautiful.

Still, as far as MacDonald was concerned, I had no way of knowing, at least yet, whether or not anyone wanted revenge on him. I needed to do more digging to find that out, and I thought I just might have the perfect way to find out more, especially if Beattie, Adaire, and Aaran were in for a little sleuthing.

By the time Beattie was out of the shower, I had a full-on "two birds with one stone" plan that was going to give us plenty to talk about tonight *and* help me find out more about what the murderer's motivation might have been. I felt brilliant.

7

My feeling of brilliance lasted until I tripped on my dress at the door of the restaurant and literally fell into Adaire's arms.

Fortunately, the evening only improved from there. Adaire gently set me back on my feet, but then he didn't remove his hand from the small of my back as he pointed me toward our table in the back of the restaurant. Aaran, I noticed, simply gestured for Beattie to go ahead of him, so I thought maybe we weren't going to have a 'brothers and best friends' love situation here after all. Still, everyone was smiling, including me, even though I could still feel the blush of embarrassment in my cheeks.

At Beattie's request, Aaran ordered a bottle of white wine for us, and then he told us about the fish that was probably freshest from the boat today. The three of them took his advice and ordered the special while I decided on mushroom ravioli in a cream and truffle oil sauce that sounded like absolute heaven on a plate, especially to my seafood-hating palate.

While we waited, we munched on the absolutely scrumptious bread and fresh butter our server brought, and Aaran regaled us with fishing tales that had Beattie and me laughing and gasping in suspense. I'd never thought Melville was much of a fisherman for real because while his book was fantastic in a number of ways it was not a page-turner, and every fisherman I had met could tell a story better than Edgar Allan Poe himself.

When our meals arrived and the natural lull of first bites settled around us, I decided to take the opportunity to posit my question for the group. "So, anyone want to go snoop around Davis MacDonald's house with me tomorrow?"

When three forks stopped mid-way to three mouths, I realized I might have needed a little more lead-up before suggesting what sounded like breaking and entering to my best friend, her date, and my date. I quickly sputtered out, "With the Inspector's permission, I mean." I stuffed a whole ravioli in my mouth and then had to do that thing where I keep my teeth apart and try to mush the food to death so that I'm not chewing with my mouth full because I took too big of a bite.

Beattie smiled and, as she always does, saved me. "Poe and I were talking earlier today about alternative motives for MacDonald's death. The inspector seems pretty committed to the idea that this is book-related, and that's certainly a possibility—"

Aaran interrupted, "But you think it could be something else, like a heartbroken lover." His eyes grew wide with delight, and when I looked over at Beattie, I thought I saw her pupils forming tiny hearts. She loved a good exaggeration almost more than I did.

"Exactly," I said. "But we don't know enough to even hazard a guess. So I thought maybe I could ask the inspector if we could look around MacDonald's house for more information about the book." I laid a lot of emphasis on the word *book* for effect.

Three heads nodded, and we spent the next two hours planning our mission, as we decided to call it because, as

Adaire said, we could all feel a bit more like Tom Cruise that way. I had never thought I wanted to feel like Tom Cruise, honestly, but in this context, it was pretty fun.

After dessert and a second bottle of wine, the four of us wandered back onto the street, a bit tipsy and full of giddiness about tomorrow's escapades. Maybe a little romance was also involved because Aaran asked Beattie if she wanted to see his boat, a question he asked with a tone so full of innuendo that even I blushed. My friend, however, didn't bat an eye before she said yes.

The two of them headed off in what I could only assume was the direction of the docks, and Adaire and I continued walking down the street next to the river. The lights of the city were gorgeous – all golden in the thin fog. Our stroll led us up and over a footbridge, and when we paused at the apex to look down at the river, I decided this was the most beautiful spot in all the city and told Adaire so.

He looked down at the water and then up at me. "Agreed," he said as he put a hand on my cheek, "with the most beautiful woman." His kiss was sweet and tender, and I returned it with equal intent. But, true to form for me, as soon as we pulled away, every question about the future that I had in my head crowded to the tip of my tongue, and I was only able to keep from asking them all by biting my lip, a gesture I hoped Adaire would think was about the kiss and not about my inability to be in the moment.

He winked at me and then turned back toward the water. "Can I ask you something?" he said.

I nodded and hoped he had clear peripheral vision because I still couldn't risk opening my mouth to answer lest all my high-pressure question pour out.

"Do you think you'd like to see me again?" His voice was quiet.

I turned toward him and said, "That kiss didn't tell you your answer?"

This made him smile. "Well, I was hoping I interpreted it right, but we do have this thing called the Atlantic Ocean to consider." He turned back to me. "I mean, I'm not asking for a lifelong commitment or something," he said as a blush spread over his cheeks, "but I like you, and I just don't do casual well."

I leaned forward and kissed him, not quite so sweetly this time. When I pulled back, I said, "I don't do casual well either, and I like you even more for asking me all the questions I was trying not to ask." The two of us would have to have a lot more conversation about this topic, but for now, it was enough to know we were both considering things the same way.

He grinned and kissed me one more time before walking me back to the hotel. When we reached the door, I said, "Thank you for a wonderful night," and let him kiss me yet again. He kissed my fingers before he turned to go, and then I said, "Hey, I don't have to worry about Beattie, do I?"

He turned back to me and laughed. "Hardly. If anything I should ask you that about Aaran. My brother puts on a big show, but he's a huge softie . . . and a complete gentleman." He waved and then walked up the road whistling.

Sure enough, Beattie was back just a few minutes after me, but she did have those plumped lips that showed she had been thoroughly kissed. And if they hadn't been a dead giveaway, the way she skipped around the hotel room would have been.

After a quick but general catch-up about the remainder of our evenings, the two of us slipped into bed, and I jotted off a quick text to the inspector to ask, as casually as possible, if we could visit MacDonald's house to see if he had anything relevant about the book. I refrained from suggesting he need not be there since that seemed suspicious.

He replied, almost immediately, despite the late hour and said we could certainly take a look around and that he'd have one of his officers meet us there at 10 a.m. "Please do let me know if you find anything relevant, though," he added.

I assured him we would and then drifted off to sleep, where I dreamed the Pink Panther – the pink cat from the cartoons, not Poirot's master thief - was traveling on a ship across the Atlantic. Dreams have a strange way of telling you the truth, even when you can't quite understand what they're saying.

AFTER A SERIES OF TEXTS, both business-oriented and flirty, Adaire and I decided the four of us would meet in our hotel lobby at 9:30 and walk over to MacDonald's house together. I figured this would give us a chance to plan our approach in a bit more detail. Plus, I was pretty eager to see Adaire again, and if we met here, I got to spend an extra half-hour with him.

What I didn't plan for was the fact that drinking two carafes of coffee would make me feel like I was the Roadrunner on those old cartoons. By the time Beattie and I headed to the lobby, I felt like I could maybe just skip down the side of the building a la Spiderman. Clearly, caffeine also made me think of every cartoon I'd ever seen, and I had to tamp down my desire to stand like She-Ra with her sword at the elevator as Adaire and Aaran walked over. I was feeling spunky.

Adaire gave me a sweet kiss on the cheek, and Beattie planted a significantly less sweet kiss on Aaran's lips. He didn't seem to mind, and with the four of us flushed with romance, we began our walk across the river.

While I'd caffeinated that morning, Beattie and I had set out a loose plan of research. We figured our best bet for finding information would be in the spaces that MacDonald spent more time – his office and his bedroom – so we planned to start there, with Adaire and me in the library and her and Aaran in the bedroom. Then, if those things didn't pan out, we'd check other rooms like the kitchen to see what we would find.

We told the men our plan, and then we brainstormed the kind of things we might be looking for – letters, ledgers, photographs. I kept imagining blackmail notes constructed from clipped magazines, but I kept that thought to myself because it seemed a little too *Criminal Minds* for the situation. In all likelihood, we weren't looking for an attention-seeking serial killer here. Probably.

When we got to MacDonald's house, the officer let us in and then told us she'd be in her patrol car out front if we needed anything. I let out a small sight of relief that she hadn't felt the need to oversee our actions as I shut the door, and then we all set to work. Adaire went straight to the bookshelves in the library, probably because he was curious about the titles. But I didn't dissuade him because he, of all of us except maybe Beattie, would be able to see if other books on the shelves were things of worth. If they were, our money motive might be firmer.

I turned to the desk and looked methodically through each drawer. They were full of mostly the things desks are full of: note pads and paper clips, old to-do lists and staple removers. The lower drawer on the left was filled with files, and one by one, I took them out and looked through them carefully. Nothing stood out as suspicious. In fact, his files looked like mine at home. Bills, manuals for appliances, and records about pets that it felt important to keep but that I never needed.

We'd brought Butterball along for the outing because he'd been alone a lot lately and was getting a little persnickety. This morning when I'd given him a few pieces of sugar cereal as a treat, he'd looked from them to me to them again and then, with only the kind of flair a chubby hamster can manage, turned his back on both me and the treat. I did catch him snacking a few minutes later when he thought I was busy putting on my shoes, but I let him think he'd made his point.

At the moment, he sat in his bag on the desk next to me

watching my every move. I suspected he was hoping I'd drop some of the paper I was holding into his bag so he could shred it into oblivion, but I wasn't giving in. He'd have to wait for the hotel newspaper just like yesterday.

But as I looked at my little guy in his plastic tote, a thought occurred to me. "Adaire, did you know that Davis MacDonald had a cat?"

Adaire turned from where he was carefully reshelving a thin blue book and looked at me. "He did? No, I had no idea."

I looked around the room, and sure enough, there in the corner of the window seat was a cat bed. "Look," I said pointing to the window. "And he adored that cat. He paid for it to have cancer surgery and chemotherapy last year."

"Wow, that's devotion," Adaire said as he sidled up beside me and looked over my shoulder. "Maybe we should look for that cat?"

"Don't you think his niece would have taken it, you know, so it didn't starve," I asked.

Adaire tilted his head and looked at me. "Do you think that woman cares about a cat?"

He had a point. "Okay, let's look around."

The two of us made our way through each of the rooms on the first floor and then, after I shouted that we were coming upstairs so as to give a potentially kissing couple a chance to put some space between themselves, we headed up and gave the two bedrooms and the bath up there a once-over. No sign of a kitty anywhere.

"You haven't seen a cat, have you?" I asked Beattie and then explained why I was asking.

"Nope. No sign of one up here," Beattie said as she and I looked under the bed in MacDonald's bedroom from opposite sides. "Well, unless you count this." She pointed to a fleece blanket draped over one corner of the bed and covered in cat hair.

"Do you think the cat died before MacDonald did?" Adaire asked.

I shook my head. "One of the vet bills was from just a week ago, and honestly, given how much he'd spent on the cat already, I kind of think he might have had the boy cremated so he could keep his ashes nearby." We all looked around for a cat-holding urn, but not finding one. "Yeah, I think the cat was alive."

"Let's go ask the neighbor," Beattie said as she headed for the door after giving Aaran a squeeze on the butt. He blushed. She didn't.

"Okay," I said with a smile at Adaire, who winked back at me, making me blush as much as Aaran had.

I didn't know exactly which neighbor we were going to ask, but given that I knew the pets of most of my neighbors, I didn't figure it mattered much. But when we stepped out on the street, the same woman who had recognized us before was, once again, standing outside the front garden watching the house. "Hi," she said, apparently unashamed of her nosiness. "Everything okay?"

I smiled and nodded. "Oh yes. We're just finishing up some business of Mr. MacDonald's. But we did have a question – have you seen his cat? We want to be sure Judo is safe." I'd caught the cat's name, and that it was a tabby, on the vet bills.

"Oh yes, he's fine. Inspector Scott took him home." She furrowed her brow but then shook her head. "I'm sure he's in good hands."

I looked at her closely for a minute. "Something wrong?" I said.

She smiled. "Oh, no, nothing. Just got my days messed up in my head. Too much Paw Patrol," she said as she glanced over at the three little ones playing in her front yard. "I love those inklings, but I may be losing brain cells."

I laughed and waved as she headed back to keep one of her inklings from bashing in the other's head with a toy shovel.

Beattie headed back toward the house. "That mystery's solved then," she said. "I'm glad the inspector took the cat. That's above and beyond the call of duty."

I nodded. It certainly was, but then the inspector did seem like a man who cared about his work. And apparently, he had a penchant for cats, too, or maybe he'd just taken it to rehome Judo. I'd ask next time I saw him, just because I was curious.

When we went back inside, I retrieved Butterball from a high shelf in the library, where I'd stashed him just in case Judo was around and eager to play, and then I joined Adaire in searching the bookshelves.

The man was, I had to admit, very thorough. He was looking at every book and then carefully flipping through the pages to see if anything had been stashed there. So far, he'd made it through half the shelves, and he didn't seem to be in any more of a hurry than when he'd started. His patience was greater than mine was, that was for sure.

Still, I started at the bottom of the shelf, after planting myself on my butt, and began to do just as Adaire had done. I was just moving onto the second shelf when a photograph fell out from between two books. I picked it up and smiled when I looked at it. Two men were standing on the very bridge that Adaire and I had been on last night. They were posing like bodybuilders, but instead of wearing tiny shorts and no shirts, they were in turtlenecks and tweed pants.

I flipped the photo over and saw the words "Silas Scott and Davis MacDonald, 1979" written on the back. "Look at this," I said to Adaire as I tapped him on the leg. "It's the inspector and MacDonald."

Adaire took the photo and studied it. "Argh, that seventies hair." He laughed and handed it back to me. "I suppose those were the times, though."

"Fashion wasn't much better in the States in those years, if that makes you feel any better," I said.

"Oh, I wasn't feeling bad for Scots. Just for those two who fancied themselves quite the catch," Adaire said with a chuckle as he kept searching the books.

"What's the catch?" Aaran said from the doorway. "You're talking fishing now?"

"No, keep your head, man. Look at this picture." Adaire took the picture from me and passed it to his brother, who showed it to Beattie beside him.

"Is that the inspector?" Aaran asked.

"It is," I said, "and MacDonald. The inspector said they'd been friends a long time. I didn't figure he meant forty years though."

Beattie shook her head. "What are they doing?"

I sighed. "No idea." I turned back to the shelf to grab another book but then paused. "That photo was hidden here between the books. That's odd, isn't it?"

Adaire shrugged. "Could have just been stuck to one of the books when it was put away, I suppose." He didn't sound very convinced though.

"Have you found anything but books on these shelves?" I asked.

"Not a thing," he said. "And the books are in a strict order, have you noticed?"

I studied the shelves in front of me. "Alphabetical by author. Not so unusual."

"Not unusual at all, but look at the shelves you haven't touched yet." He pointed to the shelf just above my head from my spot on the floor. "Notice anything?"

I stared again, but this time I couldn't see what he meant. "No. What do you see?"

"Look at the spines. Every one of them is lined up perfectly with the edge of the shelf. It's been that way all along." Adaire pointed back along the shelves he'd already checked.

"He flushed the spines?" Beattie said as she walked over to take a look herself. "This guy was serious about his books."

I looked up at the shelves again, and now I could see it. They were perfect, far better than I had ever achieved in my years of working in Uncle Fitz's shop. Every spine was exactly at the edge of the shelf, and not a single book was leaning or out of alphabetical order.

I glanced over at Aaran who was still holding the picture. "So a guy who cared this much about his bookshelves wouldn't accidentally have a photo amongst them."

Adaire smiled. "Exactly."

"But you didn't find anything else in here?" I asked as I carefully checked in and between the rest of the books on the shelves in front of me.

"Nothing," Adaire said with a shake of his head.

"Kitchen, everyone?" Beattie asked, and Adaire helped me to my feet before following our friends into the kitchen.

This room was almost as orderly as the library. Every can was facing out and organized by type, and he didn't even have a junk drawer. Still, we went through every cabinet and drawer systematically. My most impressive find in the quarter of the kitchen I'd taken was that the man actually had a utensil divider that had spaces for both dinner and salad forks. I was envious.

Beattie was swearing under her breath about the fact that the guy had organizers for both his pot lids and his plasticware lids when she stopped short. "Well, this may be important," she said.

I walked over to the corner where she knelt by a cupboard and looked at the small piece of paper she held in her hand. I hadn't seen anything like that in almost thirty years, but it reminded me of the notepaper my mom had kept in her desk and used to shoot off tiny messages of encouragement to people from time to time.

As Beattie handed me the paper, she stood up and said, "There's a whole envelope of notes like that." She pointed to the side of the cabinet where MacDonald had stored his impressive cookware collection. I bent over and looked inside, and sure enough, there was a large brown envelope taped to the side of the cabinet.

I squatted down and peeled the pieces of scotch tape – wondering as I did if the popular tape was actually invented in Scotland – off the corners of the envelope. Then I extricated the whole thing and set it on the counter in front of me before pouring out the contents.

Inside, there must have been thirty or more sheets of paper, each covered in a scrawling hand that looked both casual and thoughtful from the way each line of writing extended the full width and length of the sheet. To me, it seemed like the author wanted to give as much as they could in this small, light-blue piece of paper.

I scooped up the papers and moved them to the small wooden table by the back window over an elaborate flower and vegetable garden. Each of us took a few sheets and began to read. Immediately, I loved the relationship these people had with each other. The author was making jokes, both about life in general and about the person who had received the notes, teasing him – presumably MacDonald – about his penchant for tidiness and, sometimes, about the way he had talked about a new book he'd acquired for his collection.

D, it's no wonder you have never married. How would any woman stand up to your latest copy of Robinson Crusoe? *Plus, I don't know many a lass who'd take kindly to be set on a shelf.*

The tone was playful and light for the most part, but occasionally, the author, who only gave their initial as S, turned to heavier topics like the latest tragedy in Inverness or events in

Scottish politics that were troubling. I got the sense, from the few letters I read, that these people were old friends, good friends.

As we each finished reading our section of letters, we turned to each other. "These are sweet," Beattie said.

Aaran nodded. "I've never been one to write letters, but these read like two mates are catching up."

"Any of yours signed?" I said as I looked at the scrawling S written on the bottom of each of the sheets in front of me.

"Not a one," Adaire said. "That makes sense. I usually only sign an A to notes to friends, even on email."

That did make sense, but something was bothering me about the letters. Of course, Beattie, brilliant as she was, hit on the oddness right away. "So if these are just letters between friends, why hide them?"

I hissed in a breath. "Yes, why hide them? Did any of you see anything in them that seemed embarrassing or something?"

Three heads shook around the table. "Mine neither. So why, then?" I stared down at the paper and then glanced across the table when my eyes landed on the photograph of MacDonald and Inspector Scott that Aaran had carried in with him. I tapped on the photo and said, "You don't think S is . . .?"

"Oh, I most certainly do," Beattie said. "Now, though, we need to get a writing sample to confirm."

AFTER A CURSORY SEARCH of the final rooms of the house that yielded nothing new, we carefully arranged everything as we found it, except we slipped the photo into the envelope with the notes and let Beattie slip the whole thing into her tote bag beside Butterball's bag. He was sleeping soundly after all the excitement of watching us move around the house, and I was glad for him. And a bit envious too.

I thanked the officer outside in her car as we left.

"Find anything?" she asked with a smile.

I tried to look rueful as I said, "Not a thing that's much use to the inspector, I'm afraid." I shrugged, "but we did find get some more information about MacDonald's book collection that might help with the project we're working on." I smiled and finished with, "You will thank the inspector for us?"

"Of course," she said as she stepped out of the car. "Have a good day." When I glanced back, I saw her walk to the door, peek inside, and then lock it up sound. She wasn't a bit the wiser, which felt like a small miracle since I had basically sweated all the way through the back of my shirt while I lied. Deception was not my forte.

By a silent but mutual agreement, the four of us made our way back to the hotel and settled down in the bar with pints, crisps, and the assortment of documents we've found at MacDonald's house. I had no idea what to make of them or why they were hidden, but clearly, they were significant – at least to MacDonald – if he wanted to not only keep them, but keep them tucked away in some pretty careful hiding places.

The longer I stared at the papers and the photograph, the more I drank. Eventually, my pint almost gone and my empty stomach not sure what to do with it, I said, "I'm at a total loss."

Adaire smacked his hand on the table, "By George, I've got it," he said in an accent that even I recognized as a terrible English one. "Secretly, the two men are in love, but they can't let anyone know." He looked over at winked at me again.

"Clearly you deduced this fact from the declarations of love and adoration in these notes we have here," Aaran said.

"It's code, you see," Adaire said. "Here, where S says, 'Remember that time when Winky Douglass tried to bungy jump off the tower at college?' that's code for, 'Remember that romantic walk we took around the tower at college?'" The grin on Adaire's face was wide.

Beattie tapped one long nail on another sheet, "So 'My wife has decided she is going to grow enough leeks to feed all of Inverness' is then a secret way of saying, 'My love for you is as vast as our smallish Scottish city.'" She rolled her eyes.

"Precisely," Adaire said and then drained his pint before asking the barkeep to bring another round for everyone and then sighing. "I have no idea either."

The four of us looked at the papers a while longer until Aaran quietly said, "Do you think Inspector Scott might have murdered MacDonald?"

Given the fact that none of us reacted with a strong word of dissent, I gathered that we had all been considering that possibility but were afraid to offer it up. I, for one, liked the inspector, and I really didn't like the idea that he could be a killer.

"It would explain some things," Beattie said. "Like his insistence, despite the total lack of evidence to the contrary, that the book is the reason MacDonald was killed."

It was my turn to sigh. "True." I looked down at the papers again. "But given that MacDonald obviously hid these things before he died, he must have had a reason. Did he suspect that Scott was going to try to kill him?"

Adaire shook his head. "If he did, why hide all of it? Why not take them to another police officer?"

Beattie rolled her eyes again. "You don't watch any American TV?"

Aaran laughed. "You think the whole force might be corrupt," he said as he slid his hand over Beattie's. "Corruption here in Inverness. Now that would make for a good fish tale." He winked at his brother. "I doubt that, lass. It's not impossible, but I have to say, I've known most of the folks on the force. They're good people."

Beattie nodded. "Okay then. So what was MacDonald trying to hide? If he knew that he was in danger, why not leave? For a little while, at least?"

"And why hide these things? They're just notes. Nothing scandalous about two old friends exchanging letters." As I spoke, something chimed in my brain. "But why was Scott writing to him if they lived in the same town? That's weird, right?"

Adaire sat back. "That is weird. I don't write any of my mates, even emails, when I'm going to be up here. We just get together for a pint and catch up that way."

"Before we get too far ahead of ourselves here," Beattie cautioned, "remember, we don't even know that these letters are from Inspector Scott."

All the energy of my earlier insight dissipated like fog in sunshine. "True. So I guess we need to start there. Anyone have a sample of Inspector Scott's writing?" I was serious when I asked, but the three wide-eyed looks from the people at the table told me I'd just asked a ridiculous question. Why would any of us have a sample of Inspector Scott's handwriting? "All right, then. So how do we get one?"

Beattie drummed her purple nails against the table in what I knew to be her classic scheming behavior. After a few moments, she said, "I expect Uncle Fitz might like to be involved in a bit of international intrigue, don't you?" Her smile was almost feline in its delight, and I had an impulse to shield Butterball from her stare. Fortunately, he was still asleep in his bag on my lap.

Sure that our hamster was safe, I said, "What do you have in mind, Sherlock?"

"Ooh, I get to be Sherlock," she said. "Does that make you Watson?"

"Sure," I said. "Just call me doctor."

"No," Beattie said without a bit of humor and then continued. "What if we asked your Uncle Fitz to request a signed statement from Inspector Scott saying that the book was not in MacDonald's home when he was killed? A sort of insurance that the book was free and clear in terms of the actual murder."

I studied her face for a minute. "That could work."

Aaran shook his head. "Do we know that for sure? If not, then the inspector won't sign."

"That we actually do know," I said, "because Stovall had the book when we visited him in Edinburgh. It was definitely not in MacDonald's possession when he was killed."

"Um," Beattie said as a frown deepened on her face. "Actually, we can't say that for sure, Poe." She stared at me hard.

"What do you mean? We were there to buy the book from Stovall. He gave us a price, and if we had agreed, he would have given us the book." Understanding dawned on me as I said the word *book*. "But we didn't agree, and we didn't see the book."

Adaire sat forward. "He didn't show you the actual item you were going to purchase?"

I appreciated that he phrased his question such that it placed the blame for this massive snafu on Stovall, but really, it was my mistake. "No, no, we didn't see it." Suddenly, I was overwhelmed by both relief that we hadn't bought something Stovall might not have actually had and the shame that comes when you've been fooled over something you were smart enough to avoid. "Do you think he really didn't have it?" I asked Beattie.

She shrugged. "I don't know. He seemed pretty confident we'd take his offer, but maybe he's a master gamesman."

I sighed. "So now we're back to square one. We can't get Inspector Scott's signature because we can't be sure the book wasn't in the house when MacDonald was killed, so we can't compare it to the letters."

A sinister smirk crossed my best friend's face. "Well, the inspector doesn't need to know that we didn't see the book in Edinburgh, does he?"

"Lass, are you suggesting we defraud a law enforcement officer?" Aaran asked, his voice falsely deep with gravitas.

"We don't know it's not true. We just know it's possible it's not true. If he signs, the responsibility for error is on him." Beattie shrugged.

I knew this ruthless side of my bestie. When it came to justice, she was unrelenting. Once, when I was in high school, a popular guy pretended to like me and invited me to his tennis match. When I got there, his girlfriend from another school was there to cheer him on, and all his teammates snickered when they saw me sitting in the stands.

As soon as Beattie found out what had happened, she went into revenge mode. First, she glued all the locker room doors shut so that the guys couldn't get their clothes after they showered and were forced to wear their smelly tennis uniforms. Then, she gathered a whole bunch of friends and enacted a thorough and quiet plan to have every door handle on every tennis player's car covered in pancake syrup. Finally, she somehow managed to get the story out about what he had done to me and had it make its way to his girlfriend. When she found out, she promptly broke up with him. It was really a work of vengeance art and I had never felt so loved.

I didn't think we were into dousing of doorhandles territory here, but I knew better than to argue with Beattie about her plan. Apparently, Adaire and Aaran sensed the same and stayed quiet.

Beattie shot off a quick email to Uncle Fitz, and within minutes, he had written back to say he'd draw up the document and send it over by the morning. Beattie was practically skipping with delight when we headed up to our room with plans to meet the guys later for dinner so we could plan our next steps in what we were now formally calling our investigation. I was both excited and terrified about what we were getting into.

8

A fter I took a quick nap to try and settle my nerves a bit, I contemplated wandering Inverness and taking in a bit more of the town. My introverted nature, however, decided it was better to just stay in the room, relax, and enjoy the quiet. Beattie headed out to a museum, and I spent the time laid back on my bed and staring at the.

As I studied the smooth finish above me, I slipped into the kind of state I used to find when I was a kid looking up at the clouds. I was relaxed but not asleep, not thinking about anything in particular. I let my mind shift from thought to thought – Adaire, Eilean Donan, Uncle Fitz, Davis MacDonald.

Somewhere in that gliding meditation, a crisper thought came into focus, and I sat up. Beattie had left the letters from S on the nightstand between our beds, and I grabbed them and spread them out on the bed. None of the letters was dated, so I couldn't arrange them in chronological order. But the content of the letters gave them a sort of timeline, from when the writer was a bachelor to when he became a husband and then, apparently, a father. Nothing got more serious in the letters – they were still casual and light – but the subjects moved from the latest night at the pub to the joys of changing diapers.

With this loose chronology in mind, I arranged the letters in what seemed like the order they were written, and then I read them each again, in this order. Then, I read them again. I couldn't consciously identify what I was noticing, but between the penultimate and the final letters, I felt like something had changed.

I pushed all the other letters back into a pile and then studied the final two. The first of the pair discussed the author's young son's first steps, how he had toddled down the front walk and almost into the street before his father had noticed he was out of the garden at all. The second letter described the little boy's first taste of marmalade and the nasty face he made at the experience. Both were funny and tender, and the salutation and closing were the same. But the final letter contained the only postscript in the collection. It read:

Your niece is such a dear, as you say. Have you considered making her your heir?

The postscript was interesting, both in its existence and its content, but I couldn't put things together. Some idea was charging around just behind my recognition, and I needed to figure out what it was. It seemed important.

I knew, though, that concentrating on what I was trying to understand wouldn't work any better than it worked to try to remember a name or a song when it slipped past the tip of my tongue and back into the safety of my memory. I had to do something else for the strange barricade at the back of my mind to drop and let what I unconsciously knew come to the front.

I decided to go full-on spa afternoon in the hotel and began rummaging through Beattie's extensive supply of creams, lotions, and makeup. I laid out my plan for hydration, beautification, and relaxation on the counter and then ran a long hot bath. I was chin deep in hot water and bubbles when the information that had been dancing against the edge of my awareness popped forward like a child from a closet. Tada!

"The handwriting is different," I said to the steamy air of the bathroom. "Someone else wrote that last letter."

At 22, I would have leaped from that tub to study the two pieces of paper, streaming bubbles across the floor of the hotel room as I went, my naked body dripping onto the bedspread. Now, squarely in middle age, I knew the prudence of carefully stepping out of the bath, drying my feet so as not to slip on the tile floor, removing the bubbles from my body so I didn't have to bend over and clean up the floor later, and then sliding into the hotel robe first.

Only then did I turn on the bright desk lamp, lay the two pieces of paper out on the desktop, and peer at them. The differences were subtle, which is why I probably hadn't been able to consciously discern them before. But now, with recognition as my guide, I could clearly see that the Rs were pointier in the first letter than in the second, and the second writer had a tendency to add long tails at the end of the words, a characteristic the scant tightness of the first author didn't share.

I sat back in the chair and stared at the two blue pieces of paper before me. Now that I was certain the last letter had been written by an entirely new author, especially after I double-checked for the same markers in the other letters and confirmed for myself they'd all been written by the same person, I had a new and even more pressing question – why had someone written to MacDonald as 'S?'

I scoured the final letter again, this time paying close attention to the content. As best I could tell, nothing was different in tone or general topic, the author's son. But as I stared at the letter, that niggling awareness popped up again, and I rifled through the other letters again. There it was, in the second note – a mention of one of the baby's first solid foods being marmalade, a taste he had apparently hated. The last note from 'S' said the opposite – that the baby loved marmalade.

I felt the zing of possibility zoom under my skin, and I began pacing as I listed the facts as I knew them out loud. "S was writing over the course of at least a few years," I said as I walked past the TV and to the room's door. "S married and had a child." I turned toward the window as I spoke. "Someone pretending to be S sent MacDonald a letter, and it's the last letter in the collection, if my chronology of events is correct." Back toward the door.

I practically wore a path in the thick carpet of the room as I recited these facts over and over again, hoping they'd rearrange into a picture I could understand. But I had too many questions to get a clear image. Did MacDonald catch the slip about the marmalade? If so, what did he make of it? Did he then hide the letters? Or did he confront the writer and then get a response that warranted hiding the letters?

But my most pressing concern was about the author – was it Inspector Scott or someone else? We were presuming Scott's authorship because we'd also found the photo of him hidden in the house, but what if those were unconnected facts?

As I wound through the questions in my head, I realized that with each fact we had more queries to consider. But somehow, it also felt like we were getting closer to something, but even what that something was felt unclear. Were we about to discover some secret about Inspector Scott's relationship with Davis MacDonald? Find out some great mystery about the book that had started this whole adventure? Or was our research going to reveal something more sinister, like the identity of a murderer?

I FELT like I'd come to the end of my progress in pondering, and Beattie wasn't back yet. We were due to dinner in ninety minutes, so I decided to continue with my spa plan and spend some time on my feet and hands before doing, for the first time in weeks, a full face of makeup. Given, for me a full face of makeup was simple tinted moisturizer, blush, a bit of eyeshadow and mascara, and a lip gloss, not the elaborate contouring and eye enhancement I saw in YouTube videos. I did enjoy painting my toenails a vibrant teal, using one of the six colors Beattie had brought along, and while my fingernails were as short as usual, I did apply a light pink to give them just a little lift.

When I put on the one dress I'd brought with me and did a little curl-magic with my hair, I felt pretty good about how I looked. And somehow, surprisingly, that lift gave me a great deal of confidence that we were going to figure out this mystery – or mysteries as the case was now – and get resolutions to a lot of our questions. I didn't know how, but I was confident.

So confident, in fact, that when Beattie came in with about thirty minutes to spare before our date, I offered to do her hair, nails, and makeup while I caught her up on what I'd discovered. The look of surprise on her face was priceless but fleeting, and while she sat in the desk chair and let me do my version of a smoky eye, which was not smoky at all, I told her about the handwriting and rattled off my questions.

After listening diligently, she said, "Fitz's letter came in, so we can take that to Stovall in the morning. His signature will hopefully answer the big question, and then maybe we can drill down into those other ones."

"Drill down?" I said. "What are you a business tycoon now? Soon you'll be saying, 'I'll pencil you in.'"

"I'm going to pencil you in if you don't fix this eyeliner. I look like a teenage girl in the eighties."

"Want me to curl half your bangs up and half down to complete the effect?" I snickered.

"Give me that," she said as she grabbed the brush from my hands. "You're fired."

I laughed and sat down on the bed. "I can't wait to tell the guys about this."

Beattie stopped expertly flipping her bobbed hair under. "About that . . ." she turned to me, "I'm not sure we should tell them."

I felt defensiveness for Adaire rise up in the back of my throat, but a number of years of dating had taught me that my desire to defend someone I liked was much more about me and my history of poor choices in men than about the man himself. And it certainly wasn't about Beattie because, as I've mentioned, she has always had my back. So I took a deep breath, looked my friend in the eye, and said, "Why is that?"

She studied my face a minute and then turned back to the desk and the makeup mirror on it. "I just don't know who to trust right now. Besides you, I mean," she said as she met my eyes in the mirror. "I like Aaran and Adaire, and I think they're on our side. But we don't know them well, and Adaire does have a vested interest in this book situation. If it's part of what happened to MacDonald—"

"Then we need to be cautious about what we say," I interrupted. I sighed. She was right again. "Okay, so we won't mention the handwriting to them." The shimmer of rightness settled into me as I agreed to her point. I just hoped that shimmer wasn't because either of the brothers was involved in this mess.

THE PLACE the brothers chose for dinner was perfect for the evening, mostly because it was quite loud and meant we couldn't talk all that much, a situation that would likely prevent me from slipping and telling them about the handwriting difference. It was also helpful that Aaran decided we both needed to learn to play darts, so after we had our first pints and were waiting for our food – I had ordered shepherd's pie – the men taught us not only how to throw darts but also how to score the game using the rules of cricket. I had a feeling this was going to be one of those things I would know how to do only for the next few hours and would then promptly forget after a night's sleep.

Still, it was a fun night, and when we all parted ways with relatively chaste kisses, I was relaxed enough to fall right to sleep when we got to the room. The next morning, however, I awoke with a start as my brain flicked to the fact that we were about to ask a police inspector to sign a document under, at best, morally ambiguous circumstances.

Fortunately, the inspector agreed to see Beattie and me briefly before he had a meeting at 9 a.m., and so I didn't have to stew in my anxiety for long. In fact, the meeting was very straightforward, and the inspector – after reading the one-page document quickly – signed without any questions.

"My regards to your uncle, Poe," he said and headed toward his office. Beattie and I looked at each other and then down at the slip of paper in our hands. The S's were exactly the same, and so we had our answer. Inspector Scott had, indeed, written the letters, well, except for the last one.

"What do we do now?" I asked Beattie as we continued to stand awkwardly in the hallway down from the inspector's office.

Beattie shook her head slowly. "I have no idea." She started to walk back toward the front door. "But given that the inspector didn't even hesitate, I think we can be sure he thought the book wasn't in MacDonald's house during the murder. Maybe that tells us something."

I was just beginning to let my mind turn that idea around when it pulled up short as Ms. MacDonald, Davis's grandniece, barreled through the door of the station, right past the receptionist, and past us directly into Inspector Scott's office. She didn't seem to notice us, and I was quite fine with that, especially as I registered that the receptionist hadn't even batted an eye when she bypassed her.

Beattie must have been thinking the same thing because she said, "Must be a frequent visitor."

"I guess so," I said as I looked back into the station. "I guess so."

BEATTIE and I were due to head back to Edinburgh the next day to meet Stovall and discuss terms of purchase for the book. It was not a meeting I was looking forward to, and I didn't really want to spend our last day in Inverness stewing about Stovall and his potential schemes or involvement in MacDonald's murder. So I said, on a whim, "Let's do a pub crawl."

Beattie looked at me, raised one eyebrow, and said, "Alrighty then. Where do we start?"

Given that I knew absolutely nothing about any pubs in Inverness beyond the ones we'd been to, I decided to let the universe guide us and pointed to a place with a fox sign hanging over the door. "There," I said.

"You got it, sister," Beattie said as she took my arm and led me to The Fox and the Hound, a pub that looked like it had been there long before Walt Disney's people thought of their story. After two pints there, we headed over to The Fish's Whistle just up the street. I'm fairly sure we found three or four other places to visit, but by that time, I'd lost all sense of time and place, and I definitely wasn't going to remember any names.

In fact, we were so tipsy and, apparently, so "American," as the hotel concierge told us the next morning as he winked at us, that the owner of the final pub we visited had escorted us back to the hotel just to be sure we got there okay. Talk about embarrassing.

The afternoon of imbibing, however, did have the desired effect of distracting us from our investigation, and even the next morning when the hangover made it hard for me to even open my eyes outside, I still had only enough brain power to navigate the day without ruminating on anything more significant.

Fortunately, Beattie recovered more quickly than I did, so she drove us back to Edinburgh. By the time we were checked into our bed and breakfast near Arthur's Seat, my headache had subsided, my stomach had settled, and the questions about MacDonald's murder resurfaced. I didn't really have time to mull too long on that topic, though, because we were due to meet Stovall for dinner to negotiate a purchase.

Beattie had been handling the conversation with him via email, a fact I was grateful for, because my distaste for the man had grown exponentially ever since the possibility that he had conned us about the book at our first meeting had come to light. I didn't like arrogance much, and Stovall had that in spades. But I couldn't abide deception, not at all.

Our plan was to meet Stovall and his guest Denise at a quiet French restaurant in Old Town. I wasn't particularly enthused about eating French food on one of our last nights in Scotland, but I figured the Scots liked variety in their eating as much as I did. I'd just have to double down on my commitment to try all the city's meat pies the next day.

The restaurant turned out to be quite delightful, and I had a wonderful mushroom risotto with a lovely side salad. Beattie, as usual, had some sort of fish, and she swore it was absolutely amazing. To be honest, I didn't pay much attention to what Stovall and Denise ate because I was too preoccupied with trying to figure out if they were a couple. They acted couple-like – finishing each other's sentences and removing unwanted food from each other's plates – but I didn't see them touch each other at all, not even knees pressed together under the table, a situation I evaluated when I pretended to drop a fork so I could peek.

But when our main courses were finished and Stovall brought our conversation back around to the Sea Monster Chronicles, I had no trouble focusing at all, especially when Beattie led our offer by suggesting we'd now pay $25,000 pounds and no more. We had discussed this strategy, deciding to go in very low and cite the controversy over the book as well as our doubts about Stovall's trustworthiness as cause enough.

Stovall, after an initial flush that indicated his reaction to our offer, declined. "If that is the best you can do, lasses, then I'll just deal directly with the Library." The smugness of his tone made my blood boil.

Beattie, however, seemed unfazed as she tapped the screen of her phone, pulled up something, and then turned her phone so Stovall could read it. He scanned the screen, and the further down his eyes went the paler he got. Finally, he looked up, and Beattie slipped her phone back into her purse. "You were saying?" she said.

I wasn't sure exactly what Beattie had shown him, but given Adaire's repeated assurances that the Library would buy only from representation for my Uncle Fitz, I figured it must have been something to that effect.

My suspicion was confirmed when she said, "As you can imagine, the Director isn't inclined to change her mind. She and my employer have known each other for several decades."

I held back a smile as I realized that Beattie and Uncle Fitz had pulled all their strings and gotten Dr. Heidi Lodge to confirm the Library's requirement to buy from my uncle only.

Stovall, to his credit, maintained a professional demeanor and said, "Well, I see your position. I do have other potential buyers, however."

The man was good, and I couldn't tell if he was bluffing or

not. Given, though, that we suspected he had, at least, a passing involvement in Davis MacDonald's murder, I knew we still had the upper hand in our negotiations. "Mr. Stovall, we have no desire to defraud you or give you less than a fair price for the book." I cleared my throat and tried to look demure and probably only looked a little embarrassed. "We are willing to pay $30,000 for the book, and we will also give you our assurances that we will not share your relationship with Davis MacDonald with the press that has contacted us."

I wasn't lying exactly. I had asked my friend Marie back in the States, who wrote for a little paper up in Octonia County, to write me and ask me some questions about a man named Davis MacDonald. She cared not one whit about a Scottish guy, but she'd been a good sport and emailed me a query on her business letterhead, a message I could happily share with Stovall if need be.

A bit more of the color drained from Stovall's face, and I felt Beattie shift slightly in the seat next to me. We had him, and we all knew it. "$30,000 is acceptable," Stovall said.

Denise's face broke into a giant grin, and she grabbed Stovall's hand. "Great decision, baby," she squealed. "Now we can take that honeymoon in Bali."

And there was my answer to the totally irrelevant question about their status. I silently thanked the woman for being present because I thought, now that I understood the situation, that her presence was probably the thing we needed to tip the scales so easily in our favor.

"Oh, Bali is so lovely," Beattie said with sincerity. She spent a couple weeks there every summer, a place for her to meditate and relax on the water, she said. I hadn't traveled there with her yet, but maybe my new commissions and flexible schedule would make that possible this year. I was almost as excited about the prospect as Denise was.

Stovall took the book out from a bag below the table. She

was lovely. "May I?" I asked as I pulled a pair of white cotton gloves out of my bag.

Stovall nodded, and I gently picked up the book to study her. She was weighty, which wasn't surprising given that her pages were made from vellum. The leather on the cover was thick and soft, worn but not damaged in any way. The leatherwork was deep and clear still, even after all these years, and the image of the serpent on the front was both mystical and a bit scary.

The illustrations inside were gorgeous, hand-drawn and intricate. I knew absolutely nothing about visual art, but I could tell the person who had done these drawings was talented. The serpents looked life-life, well, as life-like as a mythical creature could look.

I ran my fingers carefully over the spine and looked extremely closely at as many pages as I could, being sure the binding was still solid and the illustrations still intact. Uncle Fitz had warned me that early in his career he'd bought a couple of beautiful books that were renowned for their images only to find the seller had cut them out before selling the book itself. "Check the illustrations, Poe," he'd said. They were all there, so I gave Beattie the nod.

She pulled a leather-clad checkbook out of her bag and carefully filled out the check for $30,000. Then, she tore it and handed it to Stovall, also sliding her card across the table. "If you need anything further or find yourself the owner of any rare titles, please do reach out."

I followed my lead and passed him my business card, too. "Thank you, Mr. Stovall. It's been a pleasure doing business with you." I stood, and Beattie and I walked calmly out of the restaurant and up the street.

As soon as we were out of sight of Stovall and Denise, I jumped into the air and pumped my first. "My first sale," I said.

Beattie looked down into her bag and said, "You think she's a little excited."

When I looked down at our hamster, I was pretty sure he rolled his eyes.

WITH A LATE-NIGHT EMAIL sent to Uncle Fitz and the book stowed carefully in our room's safe, Beattie and I decided to go out and enjoy a bit of the Edinburgh nightlife. Let me be clear, though – we were not going out clubbing. Instead, we decided to take in The Scottish Play at a local theater. The show started in a half-hour and because we bought tickets at the last minute, we got great seats at a discounted price.

Macbeth wasn't my favorite of Shakespeare's plays – *As You Like It* and *The Taming of the Shrew* tied for that title – but it was hard to pass up seeing it in its original setting. That setting, however, took on an unexpected feel when we realized that this version of Macbeth was actually a Scottish version of Doctor Who, and the castle was the TARDIS. I was a huge fan of the show, so I didn't mind. But Beattie spent the entire intermission whining about how Shakespeare was better without time travel.

"Come on, you have to admit that casting Banquo as the Doctor's companion worked pretty well," I said purely to get a rise out of her.

"You think that one of the greatest roles in all of theater—" She interrupted herself when she saw me grinning. "You're just riling me up on purpose, aren't you?"

I nodded vigorously. "Of course. It was a little jarring for me, too, and I'm not as much a fan of the bard as you are." I still thought it was pretty fun, though it would serve no purpose to say that to Beattie.

On the walk home from the theater, we discussed what we were going to do for the next three days. Beattie had to get to her other acquisitions here in Scotland, and I needed to finalize the sale of the Sea Monster Chronicles to Adaire for the Library. I had lots of hopes for that sale – only one of which was about the sale itself and all the rest that had to go with having a dashing Scotsman show me around his adopted city. But business had to come first, so we decided that we would head our separate ways tomorrow, Beattie back to the Highlands and me to the Library.

THE NEXT MORNING, I texted Adaire first thing, and he suggested we meet at his office at ten to do our business and then, much to my delight, he suggested he give me a 'resident's' tour of Edinburgh. I couldn't wait for either, but I was definitely most excited about the tour.

After breakfast, Beattie headed off on her two-day trip with a promise she'd be back in plenty of time for us to enjoy some of the city together on our final day. I gathered my things for my meeting with Adaire and spent a little extra time on my appearance.

After putting on the lipstick I rarely wear, I opened up our safe to remove the book and then promptly dropped to the floor. The book wasn't there.

I shoved my hand all the way to the back of the safe, which couldn't have been more than eighteen inches deep, and then I tapped my fingers against every side just in case the book had been upended or something. But it wasn't there. Nothing was there.

I could feel panic beginning to creep up my throat, and so I did what I always did in crisis situations – I called Beattie. Unfortunately, she must have already reached the outskirts of the city's cell service because her phone went right to voice mail. I was on my own.

I thought about calling Uncle Fitz, but while I knew he

would be calm and helpful, I couldn't really face the shame I felt about losing this precious book we had just paid tens of thousands of his dollars for. I also considered calling Adaire, but that seemed kind of unprofessional since I was supposed to be selling him the book in about thirty minutes.

Instead, I texted him, said something had come up and asked if we could meet tomorrow instead. His response was almost instantaneous. "Absolutely, but I was going to ask you to dinner tonight? Just pleasure. You available?"

I almost bowed out by saying I wasn't feeling well and probably needed to rest, but something inside me said I should say yes, if only because if the book was still missing in ten hours, I was going to need the librarian's help to recover it. "Sure. Text me when and where?"

He sent me back a smiley emoji and a heart, and I put the phone on silent and shoved it into my pocket. Then, I flopped on the bed, throwing my torso and arms back, and stared at the ceiling as if the plaster would inspire me.

I had to think. Who knew I had the book? And who could have possibly gotten in here to get it?

The list of answers to the first question wasn't that long, as far as I knew, but as I thought of Ms. MacDonald, Inspector Scott, Adaire, Aaran, Uncle Fitz, Stovall, his girlfriend Denise, and Beattie, I realized that any of them could have, even casually, mentioned the book to anyone in the world. So really, anyone could have known I had the book.

The second question limited that list significantly. Obviously, Beattie had the combination, but given that she was my best friend and had the opposite of a motive to steal it, I struck her from the list immediately. Almost everyone else got excluded because they would have had to not only get into our room but also into the safe to get the book.

So I was really left with only one suspect: Inspector Scott. Ideas turned quickly into suspicions as they zinged around my brain, and I felt myself getting more and more sure that something suspicious was going on with the police officer.

Almost as soon as that thought fully formed, though, a giant pit gathered in the pit of my stomach. If a policeman had stolen my book, I couldn't imagine what I could do about it. I briefly ran through all the TV scenarios I knew. 1. Find a trusted friend on the force, confide in them, and see what they could dig up, but that wouldn't work because I didn't have any friends here. 2. See if I could find out anything myself by asking around at the station or entrapping the inspector himself. I immediately discarded that idea because I was sure I'd draw more attention to myself by doing either of those things than I would get information. 3. Ask the hotel staff to help.

That third one seemed the most likely. Surely, they had methods of opening the safe in the case of a forgotten combination or left-behind item. Maybe that meant they kept records of the times the safe was opened or something. I felt a little hesitant about that last possibility since this wasn't exactly the hotel of the Mission: Impossible crew, at least that I knew of, but I wondered if they could help. At the very least, it would be good to file a report with them lest the book turn up somewhere.

I slipped into my booties and headed down to the lobby with my best "disgruntled guest" face on, which is to say I probably looked a bit like a toddler who'd just dropped his lollipop in dog hair. When I got to the counter, the clerk there looked up at me, smiled, and then said, "Are you okay, Ms. Baxter?"

Concern over my well-being hadn't been what was I was expecting, and I immediately shifted from upset to comforting. "Oh yes, I'm fine. Well, mostly fine. You see, a very valuable book was stolen from the safe in my room."

The woman nodded as I described the book in great detail from the shade of "sea-like blue" to the long tail of the sea monster carved into the cover, to the Garamond-style font used in the typography. The whole time, she listened with a placid face, and when I was finally done, she reached below the counter and said, "Is this your book?"

There, in her hands, was exactly the book I had just spent two full minutes describing. I felt myself flush red, but she seemed totally unfazed by my over-explanation of the object that had, apparently, been inches from her fingers the whole time. I nodded vigorously and said, "Yes, that's it." I took it from her and flipped through the pages. Everything was just as it should be. "Thank you," I said as I started to turn and leave.

Then, I decided I needed to know a bit more and fought my tendency to not make waves and turned back to the desk. "I'm sorry. Could you tell me how you came to have the book here?"

"Yes, ma'am. One of our housekeepers found it here in the lobby and brought it to us in case someone came to claim it." She smiled. "Unfortunately, we can all be forgetful at times." The tilt to her head was meant to be friendly, but in actuality it made my blood boil because it communicated what she was too well-trained to say – "Nice story about the book being stolen, but you just left it here by where you were reading like it was a mass market Colleen Hoover mystery, not a valuable rare book."

I took a deep breath and smiled. "Thank you," I said, reminding myself to act out of my grace and not my anger, because in this situation clarifying that the book was indeed stolen was going to do no good. "Do you mind telling me the name of the housekeeper? I'd like to thank her."

The smiley girl tilted her head the other way and looked at me. "Of course, her name is Maisie." She typed a few strokes into her computer. "She'll be in this afternoon to clean the fourth floor." The girl looked up and beamed another conde-scending smile at me.

I thanked her again and walked off before I had a chance to reach across the counter and grab her by the shoulders while explaining her patronizing tone was not exactly as friendly as she thought it was. Causing a scene would do no good either, and while I was sure something quite fishy was going on here, I didn't think violence would get me any more information.

Instead, I returned to my room, put the "Do not disturb" sign on the door, and tried Beattie again. This time she answered, and I gave her a quick run-down of what had transpired.

"Very odd," she said. "I even checked to be sure the safe was shut tight before we went to sleep last night. I've not latched safes in the past, and I didn't want to wake up and find we'd made that mistake again."

I felt a bit of relief at my friend's thoroughness and said, "So someone came in here during the night and got the book out?"

Beattie cleared her throat on the other end of the line. "Well, it could have been earlier. I didn't open the safe to see the book when I made sure it was closed."

I sighed but said nothing. She'd at least had the forethought to check out the situation. I couldn't say the same for myself. This did mean, however, that someone could have come in while we were out the night before and taken the book.

"It would have been hard to get past both of us in the night, don't you think?" Beattie asked as if reading my thoughts.

"Yeah, they must have come in while we were at the play," I said quietly. "So someone was watching us to know when we left."

Beattie groaned. "I don't like that you're there alone. Maybe I should come back." She paused. "I can be there in two hours."

"No, I'm fine. I'll be careful, and I made sure not to make a big deal out of things in public. As far as our thief knows, I bought the story about the book being found and turned in. I don't think there's anything to worry about." I wasn't as confident about this idea as I tried to sound, but I didn't want my friend to worry.

"All right, but I don't think you should use the safe again," she said in the sort of tone she always gets when she's worried and managing her concern with bossiness. I didn't love it, but I did know how to handle it.

"Right," I said. "I'm going to contact Adaire and see if we can't make the sale happen this afternoon. That way, I can be free of the book, have Uncle Fitz's money in his account, and just relax for the next three days." I laughed as casually as I could. "I need to get my tourist on."

"You hate being a tourist," Beattie said flatly. "But yes, I think meeting with Adaire is a good idea."

She wasn't wrong – I hated crowds of people taking pictures at the expense of any kind of traffic flow – but I was glad she thought the meeting with Adaire made sense. "I'll be in touch this afternoon via text."

"Sounds good. If I don't hear from you by 6 p.m., I'm calling Inspector Scott," she said and hung up.

I had been going to say that I didn't know if calling Inspector Scott was the best idea, but she'd been too quick to get off the line. Oh well, all the more reason to be sure I called her before 6.

9

J ust so I didn't sound sketchy, I waited an hour or so to text Adaire about getting together in the afternoon to complete the book sale after all. I spent that time planning my tours for the next few days, and while I mostly sketched out places I could go without being herded around, I did decide I'd make my way into Edinburgh Castle, even if it meant I had to dodge photos and hold my temper as people stood in the walkways.

Adaire was quite amenable to me coming to the Library that afternoon, so I told him I'd be there about two so I could take a walk and get some lunch before heading over. It was a rare sunny day in Edinburgh, and I made my way to Holyrood Park after asking the concierge where I could pick up a little lunch.

I found myself a sunny spot in the grass, spread out the towel I'd borrowed from the hotel, and settled in to enjoy my cheese sandwich, crisps, and Pepsi, a rare treat indeed. I kept the Sea Monster Chronicles in my bag and my bag close to my body and enjoyed a lovely ninety minutes of people watching and relaxing before I packed up and made my way over to the Scottish Library to meet Adaire.

The guard let me right back into the office suite when I told him who I was, and I enjoyed my second visit past all the delightful manuscripts and items that they displayed in the back halls when they weren't out on the main floor. My mother had always said I should be a librarian, and if it had been conceivable at the time for me to get a job in a place like this, I might have just followed her advice. I could wander amongst illuminated manuscripts all day.

Somehow, I found my way back to Adaire's office, where he was waiting for me with his phone in his hand. As soon as he saw me, he clicked the screen dark and slipped it into the front pocket of his pants, a behavior I normally wouldn't have paid much attention to except that I was still a bit revved up and suspicious from the book incident that morning.

Still, when he leaned in and hugged me before we stepped into his office, he seemed calm and happy, so I brushed off my momentary suspicion and smiled back. "Are you excited?" I said.

He winked at me. "About the book? Or about seeing you?"

"You tell me," I said with a bit of a surprise about just how flirty I could be.

"Mostly the former but a little the latter, too. Can I see her?" He winked again.

I had to admit I didn't mind his winks at all. "Oh, so it's definitely a her then."

"Well, I don't like to define other entities' genders for them, but I feel fairly certain she said her pronouns were she/her." His face grew bright as I passed him the book.

Carefully, he opened the cover and turned through some of the pages. His smile slowly faded, though, as he moved further into the book. Then, he looked up at me and tried to force a a smile onto his face. It came out as a grimace. "Good one, Poe. Now where's the real book?"

I stared at him a minute, trying to mirror his expression with my own, but when he didn't blink and the stiff smile fell away, I said, "What do you mean the real book?"

"This isn't the real book," he said. "It's a fake. A good fake, but a fake nonetheless."

"What?!" I said as I put out my hand so he could place the book in it. I didn't know what I was looking for, obviously, but I needed to look for myself.

After studying the book for several minutes and still not seeing what made this a fake, I finally said, "Okay, how do you know it's a fake?"

Adaire was obviously concerned, but he also couldn't help a smile lifting one corner of his lips. "It's the binding. Look at how the book is put together."

I examined the book from the bottom and studied the place where the glue held all the pages together. "It's glued like any other book."

"No, it's glued like any other *modern* book. Older books were tied." Adaire shook his head. "This isn't even a good fake, Poe. I'm so sorry. Someone was playing on your newness to the business."

I groaned because as soon as he had pointed out the problem, I could also see it. Well, I had seen it all along, but I hadn't known it was a problem. I needed to rectify my lack of knowledge here. "Can you show me a book with a sewn binding?"

Adaire nodded and stood to pull a thick, brown-leather tome from the shelf behind him. "Look down the gap between the cover and the edges of the paper here." He tapped the long spine edge of the book before handing it to me. "See the threads there? They're 'sewing' the pages together."

I stared carefully down the spine of the book Adaire had given me, then looked down the spine of the Chronicles cover I had just tried to sell him. "Oh, I see the book you have has ridges – those are the threads?"

Adaire nodded.

"And my book is glossy, like something is reflecting light in there." I set both books back on his deck. "I suppose that's the glue."

"Exactly." He pointed to his brown book again. "Now open the pages and flip through a few until you get to a sort of gap between some of the pages."

I did as he said, and after I made my way through the pages, I noticed that some of the sheets of paper fell open more easily than others. When I studied the seams of those pages, I could see small stitches. "Oh, right. I've seen this before in some books."

"Exactly. A lot of books are bound into groups called signatures. Then, the book maker uses a larger thread to hold the book together. Sometimes the pages were then lightly glued for added security, but historically, the glue was light and not really the crux of the binding." Adaire looked up and met my eyes. "Sorry, I get a little too into this stuff."

I smiled weakly back at him. "No, thank *you*. I should have known this. It seems so simple now that you explain it, and obviously, now I can see the difference."

"Everything is obvious once you know it, Poe. Now, you can't be fooled this way again." He tapped the fake book. "Forgers will have to be far savvier to fool you, and eventually, it will be almost impossible to do so."

I sighed. "I feel so embarrassed. Some book buyer I am."

Adaire came around the table and sat in the chair beside me before taking my hand. "Everyone has to learn, Poe. I'm just sorry that someone is trying to fool you." He squeezed my hand a little tighter. "I suppose, though, that this means the original has been taken?"

His tone was so gentle, but I still winced at his words before nodding. "Stolen from my room safe."

Adaire exhaled loudly. "Okay, that's good."

"Excuse me," I said. "What's good about this situation?"

He leaned back just a bit. "Oh, sorry. I just meant that you had done all the things right to secure the book, and someone has deliberately taken it."

I raised myself to my full height and raised one finger. "As opposed to if I was a negligent fool who just left a book worth tens of thousands of dollars sitting around by the pool." Our hotel didn't have a pool, probably because there weren't enough days warm enough for swimming in Inverness, but that was beside the point. "Yes, I put it immediately in the safe, which Beattie double-checked before we went to sleep last night."

"So the book was stolen while you were sleeping? Wow, that's gutsy," Adaire said.

A flush ran up my neck. "Well, no, not exactly. Beattie didn't check to be sure the book was in the safe when she confirmed it was locked tight."

Adaire tilted his head. "Why did you tell me, then, that Beattie—"

"Never mind that," I said as embarrassment flushed through me again. "We think the book was stolen while we were at the theater last evening." I had never in my life used the phrase *last evening* before, but the accent and my nerves were getting to me. "It would have been almost impossible for someone to get into the room, open the safe with the beeping code, and gotten out without waking Beattie or me. The room isn't that big."

Adaire nodded slowly. "Right. Good thinking there." He drummed his fingers against his desk and then looked out the window in front of us. "What did Inspector Scott say?"

I almost blushed again, but then I forced myself to trust myself. "I didn't contact him," I said firmly.

"Why not?" Adaire asked with only a little lift in his volume level.

"Because I'm not sure he's not the one who took it." It was the first time I had really let myself acknowledge that possibility out loud, but putting it into words confirmed that I was truly suspicious of the officer.

"Oh," Adaire said and sank back into his chair. "Well, then, it makes sense why you wouldn't tell him."

"It does?" I said, all my self-affirmations forgotten in light of someone else's vote of confidence. "Do you want to know why?"

"I suppose it's probably because he seemed so fixated on the book as the reason for Davis MacDonald's death and because as a police officer, he wouldn't have any trouble getting access to your room and to the safe." Adaire appeared to be speaking off-the-cuff, and I thought about suggesting that perhaps he should join the police force, but before I had a chance to speak, he continued.

"And obviously, the notes and the photograph shed some suspicion on him as a suspect." He stared out the window as he continued to speak. "It was also a little odd how brusque he was about Ms. MacDonald, Davis's great-niece. Do we have any corroboration that what he said about her was true?"

"No, we don't," a voice I knew all too well said from the door.

"What are you doing here?" I said to my best friend as she came in and made herself comfortable in Adaire's chair on the other side of the desk.

"I came to celebrate with you and to see if you'd celebrate with me since I acquired three books in one meeting this morning." She looked from me to Adaire and then back to me. "But somehow, I don't think we're celebrating, are we?"

Now that my best friend was here, I let myself feel the full weight of this situation, and when I did, a gush of tears sprung from my eyes.

Beattie jumped up immediately and came to kneel beside me. "What's happening, Poe?"

I took a shuddering breath. "The book the maid turned in was a forgery." I handed her the book and then asked Adaire to explain while I composed myself.

Of course, all Adaire had to say was that the original had a sewn binding, and Beattie, seasoned book expert, immediately saw the problem. "Oh no," she said. "This is a good visual forgery, though." She squeezed my hand that rested beneath hers on my knee. "Only an expert would know to look at the binding."

I forced myself to smile at her attempt to comfort me and said, "Thanks. But I am supposed to be an expert."

Beattie and Adaire both shook their heads. "Not yet, you're not," my friend said. "You know a lot about literature, and that's a huge asset. But you're just learning about book collecting. Cut yourself some slack. The only person responsible here is the person who stole the book and left this forgery for you to find."

"Exactly," Adaire added, "so let's put our heads together and see what we can figure out." He had already stood and moved to the other side of his desk, where he pulled out three small notebooks and three matching pens. He handed us each a notebook and a pen and said, "For your thoughts. Then we can compare." He then set fourth notebook and pen on the desk and tapped it. "For when Aaran arrives."

Beattie stood up. "Aaran's coming?"

Adaire tapped out a quick message on his phone, looked up at Beattie and then back down to the phone when it chimed. "He's just up the street. Be here in ten minutes."

"He came to Edinburgh with you?" I asked as suspicion rose up at the back of my mind. I might not be able to detect a book forgery, but I could spot a burgeoning romance a mile away.

"He thought it would be nice to get away for a few days," Adaire said casually, and then as Beattie turned her back to grab her purse and take a seat next to me, he threw me a deep wink. Clearly, Aaran had ulterior motives, and I was this man's fan in a big way.

Beattie was either a much better actor than I gave her credit for, or she was oblivious. Either way, she was all business and had already opened her notebook and begun to jot things down. "Let's start with our list of suspects."

"Great plan," Adaire said and poised his pen as well.

Meanwhile, I was still trying to catch up about what was happening, and I hadn't even clicked open my pen. Clearly, I was behind, and I really didn't know how to catch up except to nod, open my notebook, and put my pen tip on the paper. Hopefully no one would notice I had nothing to write.

"Inspector Scott is our most obvious possibility," Adaire said as he wrote frantically. "Then Ms. MacDonald, agreed?"

Beattie nodded vociferously, so I followed suit. Beattie said, "And we can't forget Stovall himself."

I looked quickly over at my friend. "You think he sold me the book and then stole it back?"

"He'd be the one most easily able to make a good copy," Adaire said as he slid his pen behind his ear. "He had the book for long enough, and he definitely knew you had it."

I nodded and wrote Stovall below Scott and MacDonald on my list. "Who else?"

The three of us sat in silence for a few moments while we tried to think of other possibilities. Adaire assumed what I now knew to be his thinking pose as he gazed out the window, and Beattie thumped her pen repeatedly on her notebook. I bit my nails even though I had nothing really left to chew down after my anxious morning.

When it became clear none of us was going to have another solid idea, I said, "Three suspects is plenty."

Adaire turned back to face us. "We need to put my name on there. Obviously, I didn't do it – although I would say that, wouldn't I? – but you all need to be certain you can trust me."

Beattie laughed. "But that's just the kind of thing someone who was trying to look trustworthy would say, isn't it?"

"Is this some game of reverse psychology we're playing here?" I said as I rolled my eyes. "Are you trying to psych each other out?"

"First," Beattie said, "I don't think anyone has said the phrase 'psych you out' since 1988, and second, yes."

"Well, for my part I was being sincere, but that's hard to trust, I suppose," Adaire said.

"You think?" Beattie quipped but then smiled to lessen the bite of her comment. "Let's

just proceed as if you are not a suspect unless we find some reason to add you back to the list."

"Aha! So you did have me on the list!" Adaire crowed.

Beattie rolled her eyes but otherwise ignored him. "I recommend we talk to Stovall," she said.

"Why start with him?" I asked.

Adaire answered. "Because if we start poking around and haven't told him the book is stolen, then we might as well just accuse him of stealing the book to his face."

Beattie nodded somberly. "Precisely. Shall we all go? We can act as if we've just discovered the forgery and have come right to him."

I looked at her and then Adaire and nodded, only realizing after the fact that my mouth was hanging open. I was usually pretty quick with most things, but apparently investigations were my adult version of algebra. I could only hope that my brain caught up like it did when I'd finally realized all those letters were actually stand-ins for numbers.

Beattie slipped the forged book into her bag and led the

way out the door. I started to follow, but Adaire stopped me with a soft hand on my arm.

"You okay?" he asked. "Beattie is right. You did nothing wrong, and I'm very glad – for many reasons – that I was the person you came to with this book." Then, he leaned over and kissed my cheek. "We're going to figure this out."

I smiled and felt a little of the tension leave my shoulders. "Thanks," I said, and then we turned and followed after Beattie.

BEATTIE DID the talking when we got to the police station – or whatever the police station is called in Scotland – and informed the officer on duty that we needed to speak to Inspector Scott about a book forgery. When the young man tried to suggest they had an inspector who specialized in such things, Beattie interrupted and said, "This is related to the Davis MacDonald murder. I suspect you know how seriously Inspector Scott is taking that investigation."

The young officer's eyes went wide and he stood up immediately, returning just a moment later to say, "The Inspector is eager to see you. Please proceed to the second door on the left."

The three of us filed down the hall and walked through the Inspector's open door. He stood up behind his desk and gestured for us to sit just as the young officer brought in a third chair. Each of us sat down, me between Beattie and Adaire, and Beattie got the book out of her bag, drawing Butterball out too. She set the hamster in his bag on my lap, and I resisted the urge to take him out and snuggle him for comfort.

"Inspector Scott, we need to report the theft of the *Sea Monster Chronicles*," Beattie said as she laid the forgery on his desk. "This fake was found at our hotel, but it is not, as confirmed by Adaire here, the original."

Inspector Scott studied Beattie's face and then picked up

the book. "And how did you ascertain this was a forgery?" He looked at Adaire.

For the second time today, Adaire gave his brief but clear lecture on the difference between a sewn and a glued book binding and helped Inspector Scott see the difference.

"And we are certain the original was sewn, not glued?" the inspector asked.

I pulled the documentation about the book's provenance from my bag and scanned it for the appropriate element of the description. I'd read this document multiple times since Uncle Fitz had given me the assignment, so I'd known Adaire was right as soon as he'd pointed out the discrepancy. But I still appreciated that the inspector was double-checking Adaire's evaluation.

I pointed to the appropriate paragraph as I handed the inspector the sheaf of papers, and after he'd read it, he said, "Okay, tell me the full story about the book's whereabouts since you obtained it from Stovall. Are you sure it was the real book he gave you?"

A wave of panic ran up my arms, but Beattie didn't even hesitate. "We are sure. The book was the original, with a sewn binding, when we received it from Stovall and his associate Denise last night."

"Denise?" Adaire said. "Who's Denise?"

"Stovall's girlfriend," I said, wondering exactly why that mattered and turning back to the inspector. "Yes, we are certain. We placed the book in our room's safe and secured it before going out to see a play last night."

The inspector jotted a few notes on a sheet of paper on his desk and then looked up. "And when did you realize the book was a fake?"

I flushed with embarrassment because now was the time that I had to admit that I hadn't called him when the book went missing that morning. But before I could speak, Adaire said,

"When she brought the book to complete our agreed-upon sales transaction this afternoon."

I looked at Scott, but he didn't seem disturbed by this information at all. I wondered, though, if he just had a poker face given his line of work and knew, because he was the thief, that we were omitting some crucial parts of the story.

Beattie must have had the same thought because I saw her brace a hand on each side of her chair. But Scott didn't ask any further questions about the book's whereabouts, and I let out a sigh of relief, even though the idea came to mind that he might not be asking that question to keep form implicating himself.

After he'd taken down what he considered to be the relevant details, Inspector Scott looked at each of us in turn. "We will look into this, of course, but I have to warn you – thefts of this nature, as I'm sure you know, are hard to resolve. The book could go under for months or even years before it surfaces again."

"Was that just a sea monster pun, Inspector?" Beattie asked with a chuckle. The chuckle, however, was not her casual laugh. That laugh was her "I'm faking a light attitude" laugh, and I knew it well. She used it with every boyfriend I've had who she didn't think was good enough for me.

The inspector laughed. "Completely unintentional, I assure you," he said as he stood. "We will keep you posted about the situation," he said as he shook Beattie's hand. "How long are you lasses in town?"

"Our flights are booked to leave in three days, but if need be, we can extend our stay," I said on some impulse that I couldn't quite explain. To her credit, Beattie didn't even glance my way despite the fact that she knew our tickets were nonrefundable and that we wouldn't charge anything new to Uncle Fitz unless absolutely necessary.

"I appreciate that," Inspector Scott said as he gestured toward the door. "But that won't be necessary or - to be quite frank - useful in this situation. I have your information and will be in touch as I have developments."

Adaire shook the inspector's hand, and then without another word, the three of us walked out of his office, out of the station, and up the block. There, we found a tea shop, ordered scones with cream and English Breakfast tea, and sat down to discuss the situation.

"I am sure I am too eager to find a suspect, but did anyone else think the inspector was kind of eager to get rid of us?" I asked.

Adaire nodded. "I felt that way, too."

Beattie shrugged. "I don't know, I think he's right. It is hard to find stolen books, and he may just be tired of keeping civilians in the loop about his case."

Now it was my turn to roll my eyes, but I didn't say anything. Instead, I loaded up a scone with cream and stuffed half of it into my mouth to buy myself some time. After I finished chewing, I said, "I think we should talk to the maid next."

"Agreed," said Adaire. "She might have seen something that she didn't know was important."

"Plus, we don't know exactly where in the hotel lobby she found the book. That might be relevant," I added.

Beattie nodded as if she was going to agree, but when her eyes grew wide as she looked over my right shoulder. "We may need to go another direction," she whispered.

I turned to follow her gaze and saw Stovall and Denise walk into the tea shop. A shiver ran up my spine at the odds, but I decided to think of it was the Universe being of assistance rather than of a potential murderer stalking us.

"Mr. Stovall," Beattie said as she stood and waved. "Won't you and Denise join us? We were just discussing a development with the book."

A flash of annoyance passed over Denise's face, but when

she composed her visage into a thin smile, she said "That would be lovely, dear. Please."

I didn't know why, but I was finding myself more and more suspicious of that woman. When Adaire stood up and reached over to hugged her, my suspicion turned to jealousy. "You two know each other?" I said.

"Oh yes," Denise answered. "We're colleagues at the library. I must have forgotten to mention that."

I looked over at Adaire and he winked then shrugged. I wasn't sure how to interpret that combination of gestures, so I just nodded and turned back to Stovall. "This book is a fake," I said as I picked up the tome from the table and dropped it for emphasis. I did not anticipate that the plates and glasses on the table would clatter at my symbolic show of disgust and blushed when every head in the shop turned to look at us. At that point, I blushed and shrunk back a bit.

"I assure you, my dear, it is not," Stovall said as he picked up the title. But then as he studied the volume, his face fell. He turned the book over, peered down the spine, and then flipped through the pages. "This is a forgery." His voice drew the attention of the rest of the patrons again.

I figured we had about five minutes before we were all asked to leave. "So what you're saying," I asked in as even a tone as I could, "was that you didn't know about this?"

"Are you accusing me of selling you a forgery?" His voice was sharp and still loud enough to draw eyes from the surrounding tables.

Beattie leaned forward and spoke very quietly. "No, the book you sold us last night was the original. We are good at our business, sir." The message was clear – 'you would not have fooled us so easily, you arrogant jerk.' "But that copy was stolen from our safe last night, and this forgery was found in the hotel lobby this morning."

Stovall picked up the book again. I couldn't tell if he was

trying to buy time while he lowered his blood pressure or if he was studying the forgery for some clue. Finally, he said, "This isn't a bad mock-up, the binding aside. Someone put a lot of money and effort into creating this." His voice was steady and curious now. "That seems odd to me, doesn't it to you?" He looked first at Denise and then Adaire.

I darted my eyes between the three of them and then landed on Beattie. "Why is that odd?"

Before she could answer, a large, calloused hand dropped onto her shoulder as Aaran bent over and kissed her cheek before sitting down. "What's this meeting of the minds about, huh?"

With considerable effort, I resisted the urge to groan as Beattie briefly explained the situation to get him up to speed.

"Crivvens," Aaran said. "Is the book worth all that effort?"

"That's just what I was saying," Stovall said. "The book is valuable, of course, but this copy alone probably cost a few thousand to make. Why go to all that trouble for this book?"

Denise nodded. "It does seem a wee bit odd. We handle books every day that are worth far more than this." She dipped her head toward Adaire as she spoke. "And most of those have never been forged because they are just too obscure to be worth it. This one isn't worth all that much, is obscure, and yet someone hired a good bookmaker to create this duplicate."

I looked over at Adaire and found he was nodding. "That's true. I hadn't thought of it that way, but you're all right. This whole situation is, um, fishy," he said and then grinned widely.

Aaran groaned. "Enough with the sea puns, brother. Who would want to go to this much trouble?"

Beattie, Adaire, and I exchanged glances, and then, by silent agreement, filled the other three in on our suspect lists. If only Adaire had brought two more notebooks . . .

By the time we'd finished our second and third pots of tea, we were no further along in figuring out who forged the book –

or who killed MacDonald for that matter. But it had become fairly obvious that the book and the murder had to be linked, just as Scott had suspected, simply because the kind of effort involved in this forgery seemed likely linked in the kind of audacity it took to kill a man in his own home.

"We still have to prove the connection, though," Adaire said.

Denise shook her head. "Why do we need to prove anything? Isn't this the police's job?"

The other five of us just stared at her until she sputtered. "I know he's a suspect, but still, why are we butting into something that is none of our business."

My suspicion raised its head from the depths again. "Well, it is my business since I was robbed, tricked, and now own a worthless book that I paid tens of thousands for." I shook my head. "But also, a man was murdered, and an interesting but not-at-all famous book, as you just said yourself, was stolen and replaced with at least a passable forgery. Aren't you the least bit curious about what's going on?"

Denise stood up and shook her head. "Actually no. I'm going home. Seamus?" She looked down at him as if she expected him to rise at her command.

He did not.

He also did not meet her eyes but stared at the bottom of his tea mug while she continued to stare at him. Finally, she huffed and walked out of the shop.

"You sure you wanted to do that?" Aaran asked. "Could be a bit chilly at home for you this evening."

Stovall waved a hand in the air. "Oh, we don't live together. Just started dating, in fact. And to be honest, I don't much like her anyway. Thought the book thing would do, but even a shared passion can't overcome an attitude like that."

I looked at him carefully and found I liked the man a bit more now. "So what's next?" I asked.

"It's time I use my contacts," Stovall said as he pulled out his phone. Given the serious tone of his statement, I sort of expected him to touch an earpiece and call in the Avengers or something. But instead, he simply said, "Yes, I need to bring some friends to see you. Now good?"

"She'll see us. But she won't be patient," he said as he stood.

My friends all followed suit, and I looked up at them agape at their willingness to go along with the plans of a man we had, up until a half-hour ago, suspected of both forgery and murder. But when Beattie raised one eyebrow at me, I pried myself out of the chair and let them lead me out the door, even though I really just wanted to go back to the room, eat a candy bar, and watch a game show.

10

I pushed back my urge to be a twenty-first century hermit who occasionally partook in international travel and paced behind Stovall as he wound his way through Edinburgh's Old Town. When he took one last left into a narrow alley, I felt my pulse quicken. This had to be one of the oldest streets in the city, and I was dying to slow down and look around.

Stovall, however, didn't slow his pace until he reached an arched doorway in the right-hand wall of a three-story stone building. There, he knocked, grabbed the iron handle, and pushed open the door.

I was the last of our group, so it took me a few moments to reach the door, but when I did, I gasped. It was like walking into an apothecary's shop from the eighteenth century. The walls were lined with shelves made of dark wood, and each shelf held vials and bottles of tinctures in shades of color that went from garnet to mustard yellow. It was a magical place if ever I'd seen one.

I suddenly felt like a small child again, and all I wanted to do was look through all the color-filled glass and pour together mixtures that would bring me a dragon or get rid of the freckle I hated on my big toe (true story). Instead, though, I hung back and let my eyes do the mixing as Stovall greeted a tiny, brown-skinned woman who kissed him on both cheeks before turning to the rest of us.

"Welcome to the Book Apothecary," she said with a voice that was definitely tinged with a Scottish brogue but also something that sounded more Caribbean. "I'm Inez. Please how can I help?" She looked at Stovall as she spoke, but somehow, I felt we were all included.

My friends must have felt the same way because we all took a step closer to the counter that came above Inez's waist and leaned in as Stovall explained the book and its forgery.

Inez watched his face carefully while he spoke, and then when he finished, she silently picked up the fake book and studied every aspect of it from cover to paper to binding, even going so far as to study each small part, too. Then, she slid her fingernail over the leather and then dropped the blue pigment that came up into a small bowl, to which she added a clear liquid.

Given the scent, I gathered the liquid was white vinegar, but I decided to imagine it was some sort of potion that revealed the truth of an item's origin and waited with my breath held as she stirred the mixture slowly. In those few seconds, I had gone from thinking *Cool* to imagining smoke rising up and a tiny dragon forming from the dye.

Inez's voice broke my visions, though, when she said, "This is simple blue printer's ink. Nothing special. They just color matched your original, I'm guessing."

She then snipped a corner of the paper from one of the pages and held it under a microscope. "40 pound" She looked up at Stovall. "I presume the weight is similar to the original."

He nodded. "But the original was hand-pressed."

"Oh, this is handmade paper, but just a more mass-produced version. You could get it at any good art supply store." She finally took a small scalpel and peeled a bit of the glue off the binding. "Ugh, this is insulting," she said after applying a different liquid to the glue. "It's just mucilage."

"Mucilage?" I asked as five faces turned to me. "What is that?"

"Remember that brown glue we had in school?" Beattie said. "The stuff that came in the clear bottle with the slanted orange nozzle?"

A very sharp and clear memory came rushing back as I thought about all the things I had glued to other things with that substance. "Yes," I said.

"That's mucilage," Beattie said as she turned back to Inez. "So they spent a lot of time getting the look right, but they didn't care one bit if the book fell apart in a few hours."

"Precisely," Inez said. She then picked up the book, twisted it just a bit, and then pulled page after page from the binding without a bit of effort. "They only needed to fool someone long enough to get away with the original."

"That is insulting," Adaire said. "But it also might be a good thing as far as we're concerned because it means they might have been sloppy with hiding the original if they thought we'd catch on quickly."

"Or," Aaran added, "They've already left the city with the book, and we have no hope of finding them."

A heavy silence settled into the room as we all stared at the now disassembled forgery on Inez's counter. I was at a loss. Someone was either counting on me being very stupid, or they were already long gone, which meant I had lost a large portion of Uncle Fitz's money.

There was nothing I could do about the latter option, but if the former was the case, then the best thing I could was prove them wrong by finding them. And I figured the best way to find them was to let them think they were right.

"Beattie, I think we need to act like we've been successful with our sale and see if that might draw the thief out of hiding," I said.

My friend looked at me and studied my face. "What did you have in mind?"

"Who's up for a celebration? A loud celebration?" I said.

The corner of Beattie's mouth tilted up. "I like how you think."

STOVALL THANKED Inez profusely and then agreed to meet Beattie, Aaran, Adaire, and me back at the hotel bar at 8 p.m. tonight for what he was now calling "Operation Chintzy Fake." I found that name a little bit cumbersome, but I didn't think it polite to correct someone who was about to plot an entrapment with you.

As Adaire, Aaran, Beattie, and I walked to a nearby pub to have our now curtailed but more lively double date, I asked Adaire about Inez. "Who is she?"

"Well, I hadn't met her until today, but her reputation precedes her. She's an expert at forgeries," he said. "Not making them but detecting them. She works with book collectors, art historians, and cartographers all the time to determine whether something is an original or not."

"Ooh, that sounds exciting," I said.

"You haven't even heard the exciting part," he said as he took my hand. "She also works as a forger."

Beattie and I both stopped walking and then turned to look at him. "Come again," Beattie said.

Adaire grinned. "Well, she acts like a forger when the police or libraries and museums need her help. She knows the business so well that when we have a lead about a repeat offender, she often gets hired to try and make a sale."

"Oh, so she's a double agent," Beattie said. "Very nice. Very nice indeed." She was a James Bond super fan, and I knew that she was probably plotting right now about how to get a sit-down with Inez and ply her for information. Somehow, I thought the spy might know enough to avoid divulging her secrets to a random American book buyer.

We chatted about Inez and, to no surprise to me, Beattie turned the conversation to 007 by asking the guys which Bond actor they liked the best. This was, unbeknownst to them, a loaded question because Beattie had a ranking order she used as a gauge by which to judge other human beings. The answers the men gave to this question could make or break any future relationship.

"Idris Elba," Aaran said without any hesitation. I braced myself because this could either be a brilliant answer that showed he was a huge Bond fan and, thus, knew that Elba had been considered at least twice as the new Bond or this could end any future relationship he had with Beattie because he didn't know his Bond actors. "I'm wagering he gets the role next, and if he does, he'll be the best by far."

I sighed. That was probably the safest answer as far as Beattie was concerned, and it happened to be one I agreed with. I gave him a big smile and a nod.

Beattie looked at him out of the corner of her eye but didn't say anything, turning instead to Adaire to wait for his answer. He, as seemed to be the case most of the time, was more circumspect than his brother, and he took his time in answering. Finally, he said, "Connery. But it's hard for me to know if I'm choosing him out of objective preference or because of my loyalty to the Scot."

I wanted to applaud because both men had avoided a land-mine that had, many times before, exploded in Beattie's friend-ships. Connery was her favorite, so she didn't care why Adaire chose him. But she was also hopeful that Elba got the role. If either of the men had said Pierce Brosnan, then the boys would have been eating alone that night.

When Adaire steered us into a steamy-windowed Indian place, I was glad all four of us were still invited, especially when Aaran gave me a caution about ordering the spicy dishes. "Let's just say there isn't enough milk in Scotland to quelch that burn." His eyes twinkled when he warned me.

"I'll take the spicy curry," Beattie said with her chin thrust out at Aaran.

"Don't say I didn't warn you," he said as he leaned over and gave her a quick kiss on the cheek.

Beattie did indeed order the spicy green curry, but I heeded Aaran's wisdom and got paneer with a mild curry instead. It was absolutely delicious, and I was very glad I'd made the choice I did as I watched Beattie tear up with every bite she took of her dish. To her credit, she ate it all. I just hoped she wouldn't be sick later.

Our meal consumed, along with a fortifying cider to fuel us for the shenanigans ahead, the four of us moseyed back to the hotel, where we hoped to put on the performance of our lives. The fact that we were in pretty good spirits considering the day's events helped immensely.

When we arrived at the bar in the hotel restaurant, we found Stovall had already secured a table for us in the front of the space nearest the lobby. Normally, I would have chosen a corner booth for the privacy and quiet, but tonight, it was important that we be seen and heard.

"Good to see you all. Thanks for accepting my invitation," Stovall boomed as we approached. "We all have something to celebrate tonight, I think." He lifted his pint to us with a huge smile on his face.

"Well, we need something to toast with that, don't we?" Adaire said in a louder voice than I'd heard him use thus far.

"Cider for everyone?" With our nods, he headed toward the bar and came back shortly after with four golden pints.

"To a successful acquisition for the Library," Adaire said as he raised his pint into the air.

"Cheers," Stovall responded as we clinked our pints together so hard I feared they would break. Maybe we were getting just a little bit too much into our skit here.

"Uncle Fitz will be so happy," I said awkwardly, not sure exactly how to play into this ruse effectively, but fortunately, Beattie played right along.

"He will," she said. "He's been wanting to help the Library get this book for a couple of years now, right Adaire?"

Adaire nodded. "Everyone is so excited to add it to the collection."

"And I'm excited to spend my profits," Stovall nearly shouted. He might have been getting a bit into his part, or maybe he was being sincere. I would be excited if I were him.

"How will you spend your dosh?" Aaran asked. I presumed the word *dosh* meant *cash,* by context, but I had already drunk most of my pint so I couldn't be certain.

Stovall shook his head. "I had been planning a vacation with my lass, but well, that changed a bit today." He hung his head for just a second before looking up at Aaran and grinning. "Guess I'll just get that roadster I've been eyeing."

"Nice," Aaran said. "What year?"

From there, those two delved into a car conversation that left me totally lost, and Beattie and Adaire had begun talking about her acquisitions in the Highlands and his next purchase project for the library. I was interested in what they had to say, but from the corner of my eye, I caught movement and turned to look.

There, in a corner booth, was Denise, and when I looked more deeply into the shadows around their table, I thought I saw Ms. MacDonald. I staged my face in a way that I hoped looked bored and turned back to the table. My heart was racing though, because, well, I wasn't sure why yet. But I had this inkling that the fact that they were together was a big deal. I couldn't figure out why, though. I wondered if this is what Peter Parker felt like when his Spidey Senses kicked in, but of course, I had not been bitten by a radioactive spider, at least as far as I knew.

I almost kicked Beattie under the table and pointed, but I didn't want to disrupt our performance or let the women know I'd seen them. So I quickly grabbed a napkin, pulled a pen from my pocket, and scribbled a note. I tried to act like I was remembering something important that I didn't want to forget, and then I simply slid the note to the middle of the table as if I wanted to save it for later. I hoped the plan worked.

Beattie was the first one to notice, and when she did, her eyes flew wide, and she looked toward me. I gave a subtle shake of my head so that she wouldn't say anything or look behind her. She caught my gesture and set her empty pint on the edge of the napkin before sliding it toward Adaire and saying, "Get us another round."

"I bought the first one—" he started to say, but then he must have noticed the napkin because he stopped. "Yes, of course. Help me carry, Aaran?"

"You can manage five—" Adaire gave him a hard stare, and Aaran stopped speaking and stood. Silent communication was an amazing thing.

Now, I just had to figure out how to clue Stovall in, but fortunately, Beattie was ahead of me. She reached across the table as if she was clearing up the empty glasses and knocked my pint, which still had a bit of liquid in it, directly on Stovall. "Oh, I'm so sorry," she said as she held the napkin with the note on it up to him so he could clean himself up.

Stovall was mighty annoyed, but when he reached to get the napkin, his eyes lit up, and he smiled. "No problem, lass. Just part of the celebration." He took the napkin, patted his pants, and balled it up, effectively covering our tracks.

Just in time, too, because as the brothers came back with our pints, Denise walked over from her table. "What are we celebrating?" she said. Clearly, she'd been eavesdropping.

"Not that it's any of your business," Stovall said in a tone that seemed quite real, not just part of our act. "But the sale of the Sea Monster Chronicles."

Her face puckered up in confusion as she turned to me. "But the book you tried to sell was a forgery."

Adaire said, "Oh, but then we recovered the original and concluded our business just a few moments before we arrived. What an up and down day." He took a long swig of his pint.

I did the same because I needed to fortify myself for such a blatant lie. We hadn't anticipated Denise's presence, obviously, so I was glad that Adaire was quick on his feet.

"It was almost a miracle, really," Beattie added.

I leaned forward, as eager as anyone, to hear what story Beattie had to share.

"It was the strangest thing. When Poe and I went back to our room this afternoon to regroup and make a plan, the book was just sitting there, propped against the door." Beattie looked up at Denise with her eyes wide. She didn't bat her eyelashes, but it looked like she was about a millisecond away from doing so.

"I guess someone had a change of heart," I said and shrugged, taking another long sip of my pint. "What a relief."

Denise's face had gone stark white, and when I glanced down at her hands, I could see they were balled tight into fists. This news was not good for her. She glanced over her shoulder to the table where she'd been sitting, and when she saw it was now empty, rage climbed up into her face.

"Congratulations," she said tightly. "If you'll excuse me. . .." She practically ran out of the bar.

I slumped back into the chair. "Now that was a turn of events," I said.

Beattie looked at me and jumped up. "What are we waiting for? We need to follow her." Then, like a bolt of lightning, she was out of the bar after Denise.

Aaran had obviously been thinking the same thing because he was only a few steps behind, and while it took Adaire, Stovall, and me a second longer to catch up, we dropped some cash on the table and jogged after them.

Our strange and at least partially tipsy crew made a winding line through the lobby with Beattie in the lead, presumably following Denise who was, we hoped, following Ms. MacDonald. We wove around the club chairs and potted plants, past the front desk, and down a hallway that I hadn't even noticed before. The doors were all marked staff only, and I was sure it was only a matter of time before someone stopped us and asked us what we were doing.

Until then, though we were in hot-ish pursuit of, well, I didn't exactly know whom. Denise ducked into one of the doors near the end of the hall, and Beattie charged in right after her with the rest of us tumbling into what turned out to be a locker room. There, women in pink maid's uniforms looked at each of us and then looked away, trained to not see anything, it appeared, even in their own space.

Beattie had dashed through a door at the back of the room, so I apologized for all of us and jogged along after the men, already wishing I did more cardio. This door opened into a small room with what looked like the wide door to a service elevator, an elevator that was already going up without the rest of us.

I didn't know if Beattie was in the box with Denise, but if so, I hoped Denise knew what she was in for. Beattie had trained in self-defense at a boxing gym for years, and she wasn't someone to be tested in a physical fight. Or any fight for that matter.

"Here," Aaran shouted from a doorway by the elevator, and I inwardly groaned because I knew this meant we were going to be climbing stairs. My knees no longer liked stairs.

But follow I did, and the four of us took turns stopping at each floor and running into the hallway to check and see if we saw anyone. Fortunately, the hotel only had four floors, so my lungs and heart didn't completely give out when Adaire finally spotted Beattie on the top floor and took off after her, Aaran and Stovall right behind, and me considerably slower as I tried to return oxygen to my body.

Unfortunately, when we all caught up to Beattie, she was stomping her foot and looked ready to punch a hole through another doorway, this one to another set of stairs at the end of the hall . . . locked this time. "They went that way," she said with another stomp.

"They," I said as I finally caught my breath. "Denise and Ms. MacDonald."

Beattie nodded. "I had a glimpse of them both as they ducked in here." She threw her hands up to the top of her head. "Denise looked royally angry. I'm pretty sure she thinks Ms. MacDonald double-crossed her."

"You think Ms. MacDonald stole the book from our room," I asked.

Beattie nodded. "She was in the same color uniform as the maids in the locker room."

I gasped. "She works here!" Every thread of the story wove right into place then – the theft, the maid finding the forgery in the lobby, even who killed Davis MacDonald. "So she killed her great-uncle for the book?"

Adaire sighed. "Looks like it, but we still haven't proven his death and the book are connected." He started back down the hall. "Let's make sure we're right about all this before we pursue that angle."

When he stopped at the elevator, I let out a sigh of relief, and I think the tendons in my knees said an actual, "Thank you." We rode down together in silence, but as soon as the doors opened on the lobby, I strode over to the desk and asked the clerk on duty if a Maisie MacDonald was working tonight.

"You just missed her," the young man said. "She and her friend just left." He pointed toward the revolving door at the front of the lobby.

I sighed. "Thanks." I turned back to my friends, who stood just behind me. "It was her all right. Maisie MacDonald works here, and she just left with Denise."

The young clerk asked, "Is everything okay? Maisie looked a little upset, and her friend seemed really angry."

My stomach plummeted. "We're about to go to the police. Call them if you see either of those women again," I said. We may have just put Ms. MacDonald in a lot of danger.

11

W hen we reached the police station, Inspector Scott was waiting for us outside the door, having responded immediately to Beattie's call. "I've put out an alert to have my officers keep their eyes open for Maisie MacDonald and Denise—" He turned to Stovall.

"Jenkins," Stovall said. "Denise Jenkins."

"Denise Jenkins," he said into the radio at his hip. Then he turned and glowered at the rest of us. "As briefly as possible, someone needs to tell me what is going on."

Since this plan had been largely my idea, I spoke up. "We staged a scene that made Denise think the original book had been returned to us. She stormed off after Ms. MacDonald." I figured that was short and sweet and told the truth without any extraneous details like our pursuit of the suspects through the entire hotel.

The inspector pulled his hand over the short bristles of his hair. "Okay, this time with more detail."

Beattie explained exactly what had transpired this evening, and when she said that we had confirmed that Maisie the maid was actually Ms. MacDonald, a grimace passed over the inspector's face. "I was afraid that she was involved."

"You suspected her?" I blurted and immediately regretted it when the inspector glowered at me again.

The inspector didn't even honor my question with a response. "We'll find them, I hope." He scrubbed over his head again. "I can't believe I'm even asking this, but any thoughts on where Maisie might go?"

It didn't get by me that he referred to her as Maisie, and I realized, just then, that he had likely known her almost as well as he'd known her uncle. He'd probably known her since she was a little girl, given the age of the photo and the notes, and I imagined this entire situation was harder for him than he could ever professionally let on.

I desperately wanted to help, to try and undo some of the mess we had created, so I said the first thing that popped into my mind, "Maybe her uncle's house? She felt safe there, right?"

The inspector studied me and then gave a single nod. "I'm only asking you to come along so we can retrieve your property, Mr. Anderson, without a lot of red tape and protocol." He turned his gaze to me and then to Beattie. "This is not a request for your intervention."

I nodded slowly. I hadn't received that stern a piece of direction since eleventh grade PE when the teacher had suggested I just jog instead of trying to survive another game of dodgeball. I had gamely accepted that direction, just as I did this one.

We all piled into the inspector's car and made the short drive to MacDonald's house. Inspector Scott parked a couple of blocks away and then instructed us to stay out of sight. I was surprised he hadn't required us to stay in the car, but he was a smart man and probably knew that was never going to happen.

The five of us slinked along the sidewalk, staying low behind the hedges that lined most of the yards. When we got to MacDonald's house, a slim light shone through the front window, almost like a candle, and the inspector put his fingers to his lips and then pointed to the pavement beneath us. *Stay quiet. Stay here.*

Quietly, he walked around to the back of the house, and there, we lost sight of him. Beattie was bouncing on the balls of her feet, and the three men were shifting around trying to get a better view over the hedge at the neighbor's house.

We looked so much the suspicious bunch that it was no wonder that our friendly, nosy neighbor came out to ask what was going on. "Everything okay?" she asked.

Beattie, never one to miss an opportunity, "There's a hostage situation inside. Can we stay inside your house?" Her voice trembled a bit, and the woman readily agreed, leading us to her home across the street.

I knew without a doubt that Beattie was not in the least bit scared, and as soon as we all stood at the picture window in the neighbor's living room, I realized Beattie had seized an opportunity.

The woman pulled a sheer curtain across the window, and we all stood in the dark room watching what little we could see in Davis MacDonald's house.

As best I could tell, there were two shadowy figures in the front room. One appeared to be sitting down, and the other was pacing behind her. It was only when she paced directly in front of the large candle on the sideboard that I saw the shadow of a gun and gasped.

"Denise is holding her at gunpoint," Stovall said. "I knew she was trouble."

I knew what it looked like when a man was trying to save face, so I didn't say anything and just kept my eyes open.

Just then, a third figure dashed into the room, a shot rang out, and before I could stop them, Aaran and Beattie were into the street and up MacDonald's front walk. The neighbor was next out the door with Stovall right behind her. Adaire and I, clearly the most cautious of the group, waited a moment before deciding to follow.

By the time we reached MacDonald's front door, Inspector Scott was on the way out with Maisie MacDonald in handcuffs. It took me a minute to register what I was seeing but then, as usual, I sputtered out, "It was Ms. MacDonald?"

The inspector actually rolled his eyes this time, but he managed to get his keys out if his pocket and ask Adaire to bring his car up. Then he said to me, "Please see if Ms. Jenkins is okay."

When I walked in the house, I saw Stovall with Denise's head in his lap and Beattie knelt down beside her. Aaran was already on the phone, calling for an ambulance I expected since even from a distance I could see the blood on Denise's leg.

"Maisie shot her," Beattie said as I approached. "Lots of blood, but I don't think it's a major injury. . . well not as major as it could be."

I nodded, understanding completely what she meant. "So it was Maisie MacDonald holding Denise hostage?" I asked.

"I was as surprised as you, but yes. It seems that Maisie was the mastermind all along." Beattie shook her head.

I stared at my friend for a moment. "How did you know someone was holding someone hostage?" I asked, thinking about her ruse to get us inside the neighbor's house.

She shook her head. "I didn't. I just knew that would be enough to get Snoopy here to let us in and get us off the street where we might be seen."

I hugged my friend close and then sat down by Denise. "Does it hurt?" It was, obviously, one of the dumbest questions I'd ever uttered, which was saying something, but I couldn't think of anything else to say.

Denise looked pale, but a little smile turned up one corner of her lip. "No, feels like I'm getting a massage."

Ah, sarcasm could win my heart any day.

· · ·

THE NEXT TWO days were full of lots of excitement, mostly of the touristy variety. Aaran and Adaire, who had taken the time off, gave us a grand tour of the city and even let us, much to their embarrassment, not only touch Greyfriar's Bobby but also to take our picture with him.

But we also had to spend some time on finishing up our police business. Fortunately, the *Sea Monster Chronicles* was on Maisie MacDonald's person when Inspector Scott arrested her, so once the investigation was finalized and the paperwork signed, the book was able to be released to Beattie and me. Then, we finalized the sale of the book to Adaire and the Library. It felt amazing to finally wrap up that bit of business.

Adaire even arranged, between stints of playing tour guide, to arrange for the book to be put on immediate display at the Library, and he and Aaran surprised us with a private showing of the book in its case. "Please note," Adaire said, "There are no mirrors or other reflective surfaces in this room. We don't want anyone library staff getting cursed."

"Um, Adaire," Beattie said, "All this plexiglass reflects light." She shrugged, as if she was delivering him terrible information, information that would terrify him.

He sighed. "The curators and I are aware, but we are hoping that since plastic wasn't invented until after the book was printed, that the curse doesn't know what to make of the substance." He laughed, and we all joined in.

As we left the library, I said, "So Maisie MacDonald didn't believe in the curse then?"

Aaran shook his head, "I don't know, but her uncle must have. Otherwise, why put that mirror in the room with him like she did?"

"Do we know she put the mirror in the room?" Adaire asked with a lift of his eyebrows.

"Who else could have done it?" Beattie said.

"Maybe the curse had the ability to move mirrors." Adaire said with a laugh.

I slapped him on the arm and then held on. I was glad to have this time with him, but each minute we spent together made it hard to say goodbye. I forced that impending moment from my mind, though, and said, instead, "Another question to ask the inspector at dinner tonight."

After much cajoling, Inspector Scott had agreed to have dinner with the four of us tonight to catch us up on the case. He hadn't been particularly keen on the idea, but when Beattie said, "We have to give credit for the recovery of the book to someone in our official provenance papers, Inspector. So we need the details to record it correctly," he had agreed with a laugh.

"That's it, lass, flattery will get you everywhere," he said.

WE RETURNED to our favorite pub for our last night in the city, and when we arrived, Inspector Scott had secured a quiet table in the back, a perfect place to have a private conversation that need not travel beyond these ten ears.

I somehow managed to hold my questions until we had drinks and appetizers had been delivered, but the excruciating small talk about the book and the library nearly made me claw off my own skin. Finally, when everyone had a little sustenance, I could stand it no longer. "Inspector, I'm sorry to be so blunt." No one including me believed that statement. "But why was the photo of you and Davis MacDonald hidden, and why did he hide your letters to him?"

The inspector sighed. "You found them, did you? I expected you would, but given that they are just the mementos of an old friendship, I didn't think it worth preparing you for them." He studied my face for a moment. "But I can see the secrecy might have raised some questions."

"You think?" Beattie said as she took another long pull from her cider.

The inspector chuckled, took a drink, and said, "Davis hid them after his niece tried to use our friendship to get what she wanted."

My mind skipped back to the postscript on the final letter. "Her inheritance!" I said a bit too loudly.

"Yes, lass," the inspector said. "The girl has always been greedy, as I told you, but this was the final straw for her uncle. We were the best of friends, you see, and he would not let her taint that with her schemes. He took all evidence of our friendship out of the visible eye in his house and told her we'd had a falling out."

"Oh no," I said. "Did that mean you hadn't seen in each in a while?"

"Oh, child, no," he said. "This isn't some Victorian novel, you know. We just stopped getting together at his house and met at the pub or my place instead. We were fine friends up until the end."

"But Ms. MacDonald, Maisie, said her uncle was ill," Beattie asked. "Another lie?"

"Yes, I expect she told you that her uncle was her father and that he was sick to garner your sympathy so that you might be able to help her get the book." He drained his pint glass. "She is a piece of work."

"So she knew she wasn't getting his money?" Adaire asked

Inspector Scott nodded. "He told her so. Offered to set up a trust for her to supplement her income on the condition she got a job to support herself. Even said he'd leave her his house if she agreed to his terms, but she refused. She thought she deserved what he had as his only living relative and refused to be satisfied with his generous offer."

"And he knew better than to leave her all that money since she would squander it and leave herself destitute anyway," Beattie said with a sigh.

"Precisely. So when she found out about the book, she began trying to weasel her way into possessing it. Davis caught her snooping through the library several times, but as soon as she started asking questions about the book, which she had heard him tell a friend was worth a great deal of money and that he hoped to donate to the Library, he put it into a safety deposit box and told only me about it." The inspector shook his head. "It was really, really sad."

I leaned back in the chair. "That's why he sold it to Stovall for so little. He just wanted to be rid of it."

"He did," Inspector Scott said, "and by that time, he was so disgusted by his niece that he just wanted to keep it from her." The waitress brought us another round of pints, and the inspector took a sip from his new glass. "He loved her, but he knew she was her own worst enemy. He figured it was better for her to have nothing and not be able to get herself into a deeper financial predicament than it was to get a little cash and then be in even more trouble later."

"To a good man," Aaran said as he lifted his glass.

"To Davis MacDonald," Adaire added as we clinked our glasses.

We drank in silence for a few minutes, but then my curiosity overran my good sense again. "So did she kill her uncle out of revenge or because she thought she could threaten him into giving her the book?"

"That, Poe, is a good question. She hasn't confessed, but given that we found her fingerprints on the mirror she claimed to have never seen before and that she had a forgery of the book created and stole yours, we have a pretty solid case against her."

"She did put the mirror in there then?" Beattie asked.

"Aye," the inspector said. "At least it appears that way."

"Davis believed in the curse?" I asked.

"All Scots are a wee bit superstitious, aren't we, lads?" the inspector said to the brothers.

"Aye," they said in unison.

"At least a bit," Aaran continued. "But not enough to be scared into being duped by a spoiled brat."

That brought out a big laugh out of the group, and we finished the night with lighter conversation about international flights, security check-in lines, and what movies might be showing as we crossed the Atlantic.

OUR GOODBYES with the men were difficult. We all stood in the hotel lobby after we'd said goodnight to the inspector, lingering longer than necessary for a simple parting. Beattie and I had both decided it was better if we didn't take our relationships with the Anderson brothers any deeper given the distance situation, but that didn't make the goodbyes any easier.

I wanted to tell Adaire how much I liked him, how much I had enjoyed this adventure with him, but I couldn't make any promises about the future, not when an ocean was going to be between us. Instead, I said, "I will hope to see you again," and then indulged myself with a long, lingering kiss.

Beattie parted from Aaran in much the same way, and I wasn't sure whether to be more heartbroken or a bit relieved when I saw she was crying, too. Up in our room, we both packed up most of our things so that leaving in the morning would be simpler, then we went to sleep without saying a word.

The excitement of going home did lift my spirits a bit the next morning, but the early wake-up sort of countered that small joy. It was only after the waitress delivered my coffee at the restaurant past airport security that I began to feel a bit more like myself.

We had several hours before our flight departed. We'd given ourselves an abundance of time just in case check-in or security had lengthy lines, but apparently most Scots and the people who had been visiting Scotland were wiser than we were and had booked later flights.

After we had placed our order and consumed a fair amount of coffee, we people-watched and got a bit snarky about the various items – from sweatpants to sunglasses – that people were wearing as they passed. I was so into our game of critique that I didn't even notice when a couple walked over and stood by our table.

It was only when the man spoke and said, "I prefer my Panama hat and tropical shirt for such occasions," that I even looked up. And there stood Stovall and Denise, wrapped entirely in each other's arms and flashing smiles and . . . yep, a diamond. There was a rock the size of Gibraltar on Denise's finger.

"Oh, hi," I said, not sure what else to say. "You're traveling?" It was a dumb question since, of course, they could only be past security if they were traveling, but apparently, the coffee hadn't reached my brain yet.

"We're on our honeymoon," Denise said with a voice so high she almost squealed.

"Oh, wow, congratulations," Beattie said. "Where are you headed?

"Bali," Stovall said flatly. "It's Denise's dream vacation." From the tone of his voice, I inferred it was not exactly Stovall's dream.

"I just couldn't let him go again, not after he saved me," Denise said. "He really is my hero."

The sentiment was getting a little sickly-sweet, so I decided to dissolve it completely by talking about murder. "About that," I said, "what was the story with you and Maisie MacDonald?"

"That monster," Denise said. "She brought me in under

false pretenses, saying she thought you two were forgers, trying to get one over on my Seamus here."

Beattie almost spit coffee on the newlyweds. "We were the forgers?" she coughed out.

"It seems ridiculous now, I know," Denise continued, "but by the time I figured out you two were on the up and up, I was in too deep. That's why I tried to get you to take the situation to the police. I was hoping it would get me out of things."

I nodded. That made sense. "But you came to the hotel that night why?"

"Because Maisie had a gun. She forced me to come, and then when we heard what you all were talking about, she threatened to shoot me if I didn't go find out what you were celebrating." She sighed. "As soon as she heard you say you got the book back, she bolted to her locker to check on the real book."

"And you followed her?" Beattie said. "Why?"

Denise sighed. "I don't know, actually. I was just so mad that she'd gotten me into that mess, and I suddenly didn't want to let her get away with anything."

I shook my head. I wasn't sure Denise was being entirely truthful, but I didn't care. "So she turned the tables on you when you caught up to her?"

"Yep, she took that gun and forced me to her uncle's house. If Seamus here hadn't saved me . . ." she leaned over and gave him a kiss that made me very uncomfortable.

Just then an announcement over the PA mentioned a flight to Reykjavik. "Oh, that's our flight, a stopover. We need to go," Stovall said. "Have a safe flight." He and Denise walked quickly down the terminal.

I shook my head. "I don't predict that's going to last."

"Probably not," Beattie said, "but they both seem happy-ish."

I stared after them. Happy-ish. . . I wanted just outright

happy, I decided right then and there, and if I was with Beattie, I was most of the way there. "Thanks for showing me the ropes," I said as I reached over and put my hand on my bestie's arm. "I can't imagine a better world travel partner."

"I'm glad to hear you say that," she said as she put some bills on the table, "because we need to catch that flight to Iceland, too."

"What?!" I said as she picked up her carryon and kicked my chair to encourage me to get up. "Aren't we going home?"

"Change of plans. . . Fitz has another job for us, and since we're already this far west. . . .."

Happy. I was going to be happy. "You'll help me buy some appropriate clothing, right?"

"I'm already picturing you in a fur-lined cap," Beattie said as she took my arm and led me toward our next adventure.

I leaned down to look in my bag. "Hear that, Butterball? We're both going to be wearing fur!"

ABOUT THE AUTHOR

ACF Bookens lives in Virginia's Southwestern Mountains with her young son, old hound, and a bully mix who has already eaten two couches. When she's not writing, she cross-stitches, watches YA fantasy shows, and grows massive quantities of cucumbers. Find her at acfbookens.com.

ALSO BY ACF BOOKENS

St. Marin's Cozy Mystery Series

Publishable By Death

Entitled To Kill

Bound To Execute

Plotted For Murder

Tome To Tomb

Scripted To Slay

Proof Of Death

Epilogue of An Epitaph

Hardcover Homicide

Picture Book Peril - Coming November 2022

Stitches In Crime Series

Crossed By Death

Bobbins and Bodies

Hanged By A Thread

Counted Corpse

Stitch X For Murder

Sewn At The Crime

Blood And Backstitches

Fatal Floss

Strangled Skein

<u>*Aida Time*</u> - Coming in January 2023

Poe Baxter Books Series

Fatalities And Folios - Coming in August 2022

Butchery And Bindings - Coming in September 2022

Massacre And Margins - Coming in October 2022

Monograph and Murder - Coming in February 2023

Spines and Slaughter - Coming in March 2023

CPSIA information can be obtained
at www.ICGtesting.com
Printed in the USA
LVHW081150180922
728655LV00025B/754

9 781952 430503